DISCIPLES OF THE WHIP

DISCIPLES OF THE WHIP

Susan Swann

X LIBRIS

www.xratedbooks.co.uk

An *X Libris* Book

First published in Great Britain as *The Discipline of Pearls*
in 1995 by X Libris
This edition published in 2003

A CIP catalogue record for this book
is available from the British Library.

ISBN 0 7515 3332 7

Typeset in Palatino by
Derek Doyle & Associates, Liverpool
Printed and bound in Great Britain by
Clays Ltd, St Ives plc

X Libris
An imprint of
Time Warner Books UK
Brettenham House
Lancaster Place
London WC2E 7EN

DISCIPLES OF THE WHIP

CHAPTER

1

Marika Fremen glanced out of the smoked-glass window of her office. It was only three-thirty on a Friday afternoon, but already dusk was falling.

Propping her chin on her hand, she swished the coffe around in her cup. It had long since gone cold. She could ask Gwen to make more, but decided against it. Pressing the button on the intercom, she spoke to her personal assistant.

'Gwen. I'll be leaving early today. I'm taking the Collins file home with me. I'll look it over during the weekend.' Her voice was low and throaty, carelessly commanding.

'Oh . . . er yes. Right you are,' Gwen replied.

Marika heard the question in Gwen's voice and smiled. It was uncharacteristic of her to leave the office much before six and she often stayed on long after everyone else had gone home. She had a reputation for being hard-working and thorough, even obsessive at times; one of the reasons why PrimeLight handled so many big names.

Marika loved her job. For the past year she had

lived and breathed for work alone. Her dedication had paid off. The coveted directorship was in the bag, her appointment a matter of formalities only. She had everything she wanted; designer clothes, an expensive car, a flat in Primrose Hill.

And James, her friend and long-term lover. That was what made her present restlessness all the more puzzling.

Something was wrong with her and she was at a loss to understand it. Perhaps she ought to have a health check-up, though she felt great physically and knew that she looked good.

The grey Armani suit, worn over a shell-pink silk blouse, fitted her slim figure perfectly. Sheer dark grey stockings and grey courts completed the outfit. She wore her shoulder-length blonde hair swept into a french pleat. Neat white-gold earrings were her only jewellery.

Marika knew that she thrived on stress, loving the thrill of the chase, and feeling comfortable delegating and giving orders. So why the recent headaches, her inability to sleep, and the vague feeling of dissatisfaction which coloured everything she did?

Well this weekend she'd take time out to relax. Maybe she'd give James a call and ask him over for dinner. She and James had an arrangement which suited them both. Neither of them wanted the involvement of a live-in affair. It was a good thing that James was married. He would never be tempted to get serious.

Marika gathered up the Collins file and placed it in her slim leather briefcase. As she uncrossed her slim legs, she was aware of the whisper of nylon as her thighs brushed together. The slight dragging sensation as thin fabric slid on skin was pleasant, but something she hardly noticed usually.

Today it prompted a reaction, a rising tide of heat which seemed to centre somewhere near the base of her belly. This wasn't the first time it had happened either. All week she'd been experiencing those flutters of self-awareness, little random messages that told her she was erotically charged.

It was like being twelve again, and having just discovered the ways to make herself feel good.

After those first furtive investigations under the bedclothes, she'd masturbated three or four times a day, enjoying having power over her body and exulting in the pleasure she could coax with her fingers. It was a guilty secret, something she hadn't told anyone else about. Once she'd began to have boyfriends she hadn't done it to herself so often.

Lately she'd started to masturbate again. And her love-making sessions with James were oddly unsatisfactory, but she didn't tell him that, afraid to hurt his feelings. After he'd left her flat the previous night, she used a vibrator. But even pleasuring herself didn't assuage the hunger.

She felt as body-conscious now as she had done all those years ago. Why was she so damn needy? It was inconvenient, unwanted.

Her Janet Reger knickers had ridden up under her skirt and a thin band of silk pressed snugly to the groove between her buttocks. The pressure of the fabric made her even more aware of the state she was in.

Shifting to make herself more comfortable, she knew that the crotch of her knickers was damp and her sex felt swollen and sensitive. Imprisoned by the closed purse of her sex-lips her clit throbbed dully.

Pressing her hand to her lap, she rubbed her knuckles against the bulge of her crotch, but that only made things worse. There was no time to see to her body's needs now. She'd just have to ignore the insistent clamouring.

Marika reached for her grey raincoat, grabbed the black leather briefcase and left the office.

'I'll be at home all evening, if you need to reach me,' she said cheerily to Gwen on her way past her desk.

'Have a good weekend,' Gwen smiled. 'And enjoy the party on Saturday night. Should be plenty of opportunity to network. Though I'm sure you'd thought of that. You never miss a trick.'

'Oh, yes . . . Yes. I'll make the most of the occasion,' Marika said.

She'd almost forgotten that she'd promised to look in on the author's promotion at Waterstones. Janice Clements was a new client, the wife of an MP. She'd been paid an enormous amount of money for her first novel, a lurid tale of sex and intrigue, guaranteed to be a bestseller.

How could she have let that slip to the back of her mind? It wasn't like her at all. Janice Clements was relying on her to attend and she didn't want to mar their new relationship by disappointing her. She made a mental note now. Waterstone's – Saturday. Eight sharp.

As the lift descended silently to the car park, Marika stared through the glass and chrome lift shaft which was attached to the outside of the building.

London's Dockland took on an almost fairytale magic at this time of day. The deep purple sky formed a backdrop to the glowing towers of glass and steel, which were reflected in the muddy waters of the Thames. Pin-points of light on the Isle of Dogs looked like christmas-tree decorations.

In the car park she approached her blue BMW, her heels clicking on the concrete. Recessed lamps cast a bluish light over the lines of gleaming cars and gave the concrete pillars a stark beauty. She disliked car parks. They were sterile, anonymous, a bit threatening.

'Miss Fremen?'

The voice made her jump. She hadn't heard the man approach. He was very tall and slim, dressed in something dark and well cut, expensive-looking. Immediately she was on her guard. He was hardly likely to call her by name if he meant to mug her, but she slowed warily anyway, her fingers reaching for the personal alarm cylinder which was attached to her key ring.

'What do you want?' she said.

The man smiled. She judged him to be in his late thirties. His hair was dark and close-cropped. He exuded confidence and self-possession.

'You're forthright. I like that. And beautiful too. He wasn't lying.'

'Who said those things?'

He ignored her question.

'I'd like to give you this.' He held out his hand. Covering his palm was a flat, black velvet box.

'Is this some kind of joke?' Marika said coldly. 'I don't know you. Why would you give me anything?'

The man smiled again, showing very white, even teeth. His face was lean, with high cheekbones. There was a rakish charm about him and something implacable in his calm dark eyes.

She felt instinctively that he could be dangerous.

He was very good-looking, she decided and was annoyed at the quick flare of interest. He seemed to sense it and she saw an answering response in his eyes. His gaze flicked over her, slowly and insolently.

'This is something you'll come to value,' he said softly. 'Take it.'

Marika stiffened, suddenly aware of the tension between the two of them. Her earlier state hadn't entirely subsided. As she took a step backwards, the cool silk of her knickers brushed against her sex, which seemed to flutter in response. In her belly a hot, deep throbbing began.

Lord, all she could think about was what he'd look like naked. She imagined the flat planes of his chest, the muscles pushing against the smooth skin, his hard, flat belly and his cock, rearing up potently from the cluster of black curls at his groin.

The starkness of the imagery shocked her. She had never had such an immediate physical response to a stranger. The man could not have known what she was thinking, but Marika felt the guilty colour rush into her face.

'Leave me alone, please. You must have made a mistake,' she said, with a calmness she didn't feel.

He shook his head. 'No mistake. And I assure you that this is deadly serious.' His voice was deep and well modulated.

She recognised the tones of someone who was used to getting their own way. Someone like herself.

'It's just a box,' he said. 'I want you to have it. That's all. No strings. No explanations.'

His tone hadn't changed. He seemed certain that

she'd take the box. Suddenly she was angry. Who did he think she was, trying to manipulate her? She hated having responded to him with that shameful surge of lust.

'This is ridiculous,' she snapped. 'I don't know you. And I don't want your gifts. If you want to talk to me make an appointment at my office. Now stand aside.'

He smiled slowly. 'I'm afraid I cant do that.'

Cloak and dagger, like a bad film, she thought. He seemed to have got his script straight out of Raymond Chandler. She was tempted to tell him to go straight to hell, but he stood between her and the car. Although slim he looked very solid.

The man waited silently, watching her reactions. His dark gaze unnerved her. She felt a trickle of icy sweat run down the inside of her silk blouse.

He didn't look like a madman, but you could never be sure. Her throat began to dry with alarm. She decided to humour him.

'OK. You just want to give me the box?' she said evenly, surprised that her voice came out as anything more than a croak. 'That's really all?'

'That's all.'

'Put it on the car,' she said.

'As you wish.' Leaning forward he placed the box on the bonnet of the BMW. He smiled again. 'I just wanted to be sure that I delivered it to you direct. There must be no mistake. I'll bid you good night, Miss Fremen.'

Turning on his heel, the man walked rapidly towards the stairs which led to the lower level. Marika watched him until he was out of sight, then she unlocked the car and slipped into the driver's seat.

Who the hell was he? And how had he got past security? Her hands were shaking and she gripped the steering wheel to steady them. Through the windscreen she saw the black box, its opulent velvet reflected in the gleaming blue bonnet. It was the sort of box expensive jewellery came in. And large enough to hold a small bomb.

She was tempted to drive straight out of the car park and leave the box where it fell, but curiosity got the better of her. Come on, you're being melodramatic, she told herself. The man had known who she was. He had been polite, his manner cool, quite deliberately neutral.

Making up her mind, Marika opened the door, scooped up the box and placed it on the front seat. She was too spooked to open it here. She'd wait until she was safely inside her flat, with a Johnny Walker Black Label and ice in her hand.

Starting up the BMW she headed for the ramp, the rubber of the tyres squealing in protest as she swung the car in a tight half circle.

Marika pursed her lips and let out a long slow whistle. The box lay open on the glass-topped coffee table.

Nestling in the folds of deep red satin was a pendant. The heavy gold chain was curled snake-like around an oval of jet, surrounded by pearls.

She lifted the pendant, feeling its weight and running her fingertips across the smooth surface of the unmarked jet. The pearls had a wonderful creamy lustre. As she turned them this way and that she saw peach and pink lights in their depths. They were real, not cultured. She was puzzled. The plain jet oval seemed incongruous against the richness of the gold and pearls.

Somehow she sensed that the pendant was incomplete. It needed some final decoration to give it a unique character. She didn't know how she knew this, but she knew that she was right. There was nothing else, no clue to who had sent the pendant or why.

Then, under the crumpled red satin, she found a small black card. There was a telephone number, embossed in gold.

She looked at the card for a long time. It wasn't a London number. The gold lettering against the black looked classy, mysterious. She was intrigued, as no doubt she was meant to be. The whole scenario, the meeting in the car park, it was a set-up, designed to arouse her interest.

She pressed her lips together. One thing she did know. No one gave you anything for free in this life. There had to be a pay-off. The pendant was expensive, distinctive. Someone wanted something from her; someone who was confident of her response.

Marika took a sip of the whisky. One thing she hated was to be manipulated or taken by surprise by anything. In all of her business dealings *she* was in control. Her private life echoed the fact. She loved order in everything. Neat lines of figures on a page, matching colours, her spotless flat decorated in almost Spartan good taste.

She drained her glass and poured another drink, topping it up with water. Whoever her mysterious admirer was, he was going to be disappointed. She certainly had no intention of phoning that number. If some rich, bored playboy wanted to play games that was his affair. She didn't have to go along with him.

Leaving the box lying on the coffee table, she

ran a bath. She undressed, then removed her make-up and unpinned her hair. While the bath filled, she washed her hair and swathed it in a towel.

Easing herself into the bath with a sigh, she soaked in the foamy water. With a conscious effort she let the tension go out of her body. It had been a strange ending to the day and she just wanted to forget everything for a while. The whisky imparted a pleasant haze to her perceptions. Breathing in the fragrant steam rising around her, she closed her eyes.

But somehow he was there, the dark, nameless man who had stepped silently out of the shadows in the car park.

With an effort she cleared her mind, concentrating on her breathing and clenching then relaxing her muscles; exercise techniques she used to unwind after a hard day's work.

The bath ought to have been soothing, but the perfumed water caressed her sensitized skin like hot silk. She squeezed water over her shoulders and allowed it to trickle over her breasts.

Despite her efforts she couldn't help but be aware of the state she was in. The gnawing hunger deep within her hadn't gone away, it had merely subsided for a time.

As she soaped them, her nipples gathered into red-brown cones. She trailed her fingertips over them, idly at first, then with more purpose.

Her nipples had always been sensitive and prone to becoming erect without the slightest stimulus. They were large and prominent, embarrassingly so. She always wore a bra, or the dark areolae showed through fine fabrics. The hardened stems even poked against the woollen shirts and cashmere sweaters, forming visible peaks in the fabric. She would have loved to go bra-less, but was too self-conscious to do so.

As she caressed her nipples they lengthened and hardened. She pinched and rolled them, biting her bottom lip as they awoke under her fingers. Little slivers of sensation radiated downwards, finding an echo in the ticking between her thighs. She smoothed her hands down to the slight pout of her belly, stroking and kneading the warm wet skin.

Now she didn't try to fight the pleasure that was spreading through her. Instead, she indulged herself.

Throwing back her turbanned head, she rested it on the bath cushion and parted her legs. Drawing up her knees, she let her thighs fall open and slipped her hand into the soapy wetness of her vulva.

The first touch on her thickened sex-lips made her gasp. She had been on heat all day and the incident in the car park had added the spice of danger to her ardour. As she stroked her clitoris, smoothing the little hood of flesh up towards her stomach, she began to fantasise.

She pictured the face of the man in the car park. Lean and dark, with those incredible high cheekbones. A dart of pure lust speared her as she imagined him looming over her, a sardonic smile on his face.

Marika moaned softly. Her clitoris was so swollen it was a firm little bud. Circling the jutting nub of flesh, she varied the pressure, closing her eyes as the sexual tension built within her.

Her whole sex was puffed up with wanting, the flesh of it slippery and heated. Thrusting two fingers inside her vagina, she worked them back and forth, curving them up and pulling against the inner walls behind her clit. The pad of sensitive flesh there seemed to vibrate to her touch.

Inside she was soft and liquid, the fleshy walls clinging to her fingers. Her juices flowed around her knuckles, mingling with the scented bubbles and bath water. She imagined the man in the car park grasping her and dragging her out of the bath.

He held her around the waist, pushing her forward so that her hair brushed the bottom of the bath. The cold enamelled rim pressed into her stomach and her buttocks were made to gape as he pressed his knee between her thighs, forcing them open.

As Marika rubbed hard and rhythmically, she thought of his stout cock-head, nudging against her vagina.

'You beautiful bitch,' he said, in her imagination. 'I'm going to make you come.'

She felt open, receptive, longing for the feeling of hard, male flesh inside her. Her fingers plunged deeply inside her, slick now and coated with her pearly juices. With her other hand she pinched her clitoris, wanting to feel a more violent pleasure than her usual gentle stroking and manipulation.

The spiked pleasure, the soreness and the unusual wetness of her vagina all coalesced into a single pulsing heat. Oh God, her imaginary lover was plunging into her, rimming her dripping sex with his swollen cock.

'You want it hot and hard. I know you do,' he grated. 'Press yourself back against me.'

With a groan working up in her throat, Marika climaxed. Her womb contracted and the pulsings were deep and satisfying, going on and on. She shuddered and bucked against her hand. But one climax wasn't enough, she continued to rub at her swollen sex, pinching her nipples, until she came again and again.

Afterwards, she lay back in the warm water, feeling it lapping against her breasts and shoulders. Her mind was a riot of confusion.

What was happening to her? The unusual desperation, the erotic fantasies were new to her. She had rarely masturbated so wantonly, so luxuriously. On the occasions when she did, she thought of James and his gentle, rather diffident love-making. Her orgasms were usually gentle too, sweet contractions followed by a satisfying after-glow.

Nothing like the wickedly wrenching pleasure she'd just experienced. It had felt like she was dissolving into pure pleasure. She didn't recognise herself.

The image of the stranger manhandling her, possessing her, plunging into her, had added a new element to her fantasies. She realised that she'd become strongly aroused by the incident in the car park. In her already heightened state, she'd fixated on the messenger.

God, she must be twisted, getting off on the air of menace that surrounded the man. In fact he hadn't been all that threatening, now that she came to think about it. He *was* devastatingly attractive. It was more the thought of what might have happened, what she wanted to happen, that had driven her to fantasise about him.

He was the first man she was really interested

in for a long time. The very antithesis of James. James was comfort, warmth, order. The other man was excitement, danger, the unknown. She realised that she hadn't thought to ask his name. And now she wished that she had.

She felt guilty, as if she'd betrayed James somehow. Then she smiled, how stupid. He'd never know if she didn't tell him. The harmless fantasy couldn't hurt anyone. And she'd probably never see the man again. Unless . . . She could telephone the number on the black card.

No. Impossible. Too dangerous, too risky.

Marika's hands shook slightly as she dried herself carefully and shrugged on a white towelling robe, before padding into the adjoining bedroom. The decor was predominantly grey-blue. Pools of light from blue-shaded, art deco lamps spread a golden glow over the room.

She sat on a chaise-longue and smoothed body lotion over her limbs. Her favourite perfume filled the bedroom. Rubbing at her hair with a towel, she left it to lie in a damp tangle over her shoulders. She decided to make coffee and skim over the Collins file before cooking herself some pasta.

The open box on the coffee table drew her eye the moment she stepped back into the sitting-room. Somehow she had hoped that it would have disappeared, even though she knew that was impossible. The whole incident in the car park had the quality of a dream.

The pendant wasn't going to go away. It was a potent reminder of a disquieting incident, a problem she must deal with. There had to be a way to address this. While she made herself coffee, she weighed the possibilities.

Could someone have sent her a surprise present? James? She didn't think so, it wasn't his style, but it was just possible. She had to discount him first. He answered the phone on the third ring.

'Marika? What a pleasant surprise. I wasn't expecting you to call.' His voice sounded warm and comfortable, as it always did. But she detected a note of wariness. His wife was probably back from her business trip.

'I know,' she said, deciding to make this brief. 'I wanted to talk to you. You haven't . . . sent me anything, have you?'

He laughed. 'No. Would you like me to? Have I forgotten your birthday or something?'

She laughed too. 'No. That was in December. Remember?'

'What's this about then?' He was amused. She pictured his face, strong-featured with creases around his blue eyes, the grey wings at his temples. 'Is it just an excuse to phone me? I can't come over right now. It's a bit difficult . . .'

'That's not why I rang,' she said, more abruptly than she meant to. 'I didn't expect that you could. It's just that someone sent me a present. I thought it might be you.'

His voice was puzzled. 'What sort of a present?'

She felt suddenly hesitant. For some reason she didn't want to tell him about the pendant. She forced another laugh.

'Well if you'd sent me something, you'd know what it was, wouldn't you?'

'What's this, a riddle? Are you telling me that someone sent you a gift and you don't know who it's from? It's probably an office prank. Shove it back in the post with "not known" scrawled on the front.'

'Yes. You're right, of course,' she said, smiling at the way he had assumed she'd received a parcel through the post.

How odd. She thought James knew her fairly well. He ought to have realised that she wasn't the sort of women whom people played pranks on. She had never phoned him for reassurance before either. For just a moment she was disappointed by his lack of interest. He wasn't even curious about what the 'gift' was.

'Look, I'm sorry to bother you with this,' she said, her tone one of forced lightness. 'It's so silly really. I knew it couldn't have been you. But I just wanted to be certain. Have to go now. I've work to do. I'll see you tomorrow?'

'Right. The Waterstone's thing. Shall I pick you up from the flat?'

'I'm not sure if I'm going, James. I think I have the start of a cold or something. Let me get back to you on that. OK? Bye for now.'

She replaced the receiver, slowly. What on earth had possessed her to say that? She felt perfectly healthy and she knew that she definitely *was* going to Janice Clements's party.

And then she knew why she had put James off going with her to Waterstone's. Whoever had sent the pendant had to know something about her; at the very least, her name and where she worked. That pointed to some sort of involvement with a client.

Of course. She felt stupid now for bothering James. Why hadn't she seen it sooner? There had to be a business connection to this whole charade.

PrimeLight was very prestigious and she had a reputation for being choosy about the clients she represented. Some of them would go to great lengths to gain her attention. She laughed with relief. There was nothing sinister about this at all.

The pendant, the mysterious man in the car park, the cryptic message – it was all a stunt. She had only to phone that number and a prospective client would answer.

She glanced towards the coffee table where the black card lay on the glass top, a small square of midnight with gold lettering.

In the box, on its bed of crumpled scarlet, the pendant glowed dully. It was beautifully crafted and obviously expensive. Whoever could afford to give away something like that as a gimmick had to be worth courting. She felt a frisson of excitement, the gut feeling she always experienced with an imminent deal.

Reaching out confidently, she picked up the black card and began to dial.

CHAPTER 2

As soon as he answered Marika knew that she was mistaken. He wasn't a client after all.

'Ah, Miss Fremen. I've been expecting you to call.' The voice was silky smooth, confident. Perfectly in control of the situation.

She recognised the voice at once. It was him, the 'messenger' from the car park. Only she knew with bone-deep certainty that he was the instigator, not the errand boy. She decided to be direct.

'Who are you? What do you want?' she said coldly.

She could tell that he was smiling. His face appeared in her mind. The dark, impenetrable eyes, and perfect white teeth. What would he think if he knew that she'd brought herself to orgasm while conjuring his image?

He ignored her question.

'Have you a pen? Then take down this address. Come here at once. And wear the pendant.'

'Wait!' she said, sensing that he was about to hang up. Scribbling the address on a memo pad while she talked, she said, 'I don't take kindly to being told what to do. What's this about? Why should I do as you ask?'

'You don't have to do anything,' he said coolly. 'It's your choice.'

We both know that I'll go, she thought. This is part of some elaborate game. But he knows the rules and I don't. Well she wasn't going to let him think that he was totally in control.

'At least tell me your name,' she said.

There was a pause and she realised that she was holding her breath, willing him to tell her. She sensed his resistance.

'Your name,' she repeated. 'Or I swear I'll tear up this address.'

There was another pause. She listened to his breathing, slow and measured. Her palm felt damp against the phone.

'Oh I don't think you will,' he said. 'We've marked you out as a woman who enjoys a challenge. Look inside yourself, Miss Fremen. See the dark void, the emptiness? Are you prepared to take a risk and look for something to fill that place? Don't try to pretend that you're perfectly happy with your life.'

Marika's knuckles turned white. How could he know about that? How could anyone know?

'You must tell me who you are,' she whispered.

'Must?' His voice was cool, amused. 'That's not a word I respond to.'

There was another pause. The silence seemed to reach out to her. She sensed that he was waiting, anticipating her response. And, somehow, she knew what she had to say.

It cost her some effort.

'Please . . . .' she said, horrified at the smallness of her voice. It didn't sound like anyone she knew. 'Please. Will you tell me?'

'That's better. Now that wasn't so difficult, was it?'

No one spoke to her like that. She fought the urge to swear at him, knowing that it would do no good. Was he going to tell her his name, or was this another of his games?

'Stone,' he said, softly. And hung up.

She stood looking down at the phone, gripped by mixed emotions. Uppermost was triumph. He'd given her his name and she sensed how reluctant he had been to do so. But she had almost begged him for that privilege.

Just the sound of his voice made her react in a way that was totally out of character. Instead of the hard-nosed businesswoman, she felt gauche, unsure of herself. It was extraordinary. No man ought to be able to make her feel that way.

'Stone,' she said aloud.

It must be a surname. It suited him. An unusual name for an arrogant bastard. She couldn't wait to meet him again. Perhaps face to face she'd be able to cope with him, be her usual poised self.

The address was outside London. It would take her two hours to drive there, given the Friday evening traffic. Stone might be a prospective client even yet. One thing was certain. He was playing her like a fish on a line and he damn well knew it.

By the time Marika had dried her hair and applied make-up, the effects of the whisky and water had worn off.

She dressed carefully in a rust silk sheath dress and her favourite handmade shoes. Brushing out her hair, she secured it at the nape with a matching ribbon. The pendant hung at her chest, just above the start of her cleavage. It was an unfamiliar weight. She did not normally wear necklaces.

Shrugging on a cream linen jacket, she left the flat. As the BMW nosed through the London traffic, she concentrated on driving, trying to order her thoughts. It was no use. She was too strung out to think clearly. The nervous tension seemed to have settled into a tight ball in her stomach.

Popping a cassette into the player, she turned up the sound and let the haunting voice of Roy Orbison wash over her as she drove. The traffic flow lightened as she headed up the Finchley Road into Hendon Way. Soon she was entering the slip road to the M1.

Glancing at her watch, she saw that it was nearing eight as she approached the signpost for Newport Pagnell. The butterflies in her stomach were having a ball.

She realised that she was hungry. The last thing she ate was a tuna salad sandwich and an apple. That had been around one p.m. She could have stopped at a pub, but she knew that if she swallowed a single mouthful she'd be sick. Besides, she was nearly there.

Glancing down at the scrap of paper with the address, she absorbed the directions she'd scribbled next to it. The house was on the outskirts of a village. Ah, there was the turn-off now.

She swung a left and eased the car round the curve of a bend. Stone pillars topped with lions marked the entrance to a private road. At the end of the road was a pair of tall, wrought-iron gates.

She cruised up to them slowly. As she approached, they swung open.

Obviously she was expected. The red brick façade of a large Elizabethan country house came into view as she drove up a tree-lined drive. The moon was visible between the trees. Elongated shadows panned across the bonnet of her car. Gravel crunched under the tyres as she drew to a halt, parking beside a stone fountain.

Marika took a few moments to compose herself before getting out of the car. She checked her make-up, smoothed a hand over her hair, and briefly touched the pendant. The jet felt warm to the touch, as if it had absorbed her body heat. Taking a deep breath she strode towards the studded oak front door and lifted the brass knocker.

After a few seconds a woman opened the door. She was young and pretty and dressed in a black and white uniform. Marika smiled encouragingly.

'I'm expected,' she said.

The woman didn't smile. She glanced at Marika's pendant.

'Of course,' she said, opening the door wide. 'Won't you come in?'

Marika walked into a darkly panelled hall. There were expensive Persian rugs covering the uneven oak floor-boards. A number of rooms led off the hall; all of the doors were closed. In the distance she could hear the muted murmur of voices and laughter. The house smelt of age and lavender polish.

She took a step forward, expecting that Stone would come to meet her at any moment.

Glancing around, she absorbed details of the decor. The paintings on the walls seemed to be originals, the furniture contemporary with the house.

She hadn't been mistaken about one thing. Her mysterious, prospective 'client' was certainly rich. Probably someone connected with the arts. She had many connections in that area herself, but she had never heard of anyone called Stone.

'Won't you go up,' the woman said. She indicated the staircase which swept up to a second floor. 'They're waiting for you.'

Marika climbed the stairs. Still no one came out to welcome her. The woman who had let her into the house had disappeared. She began to feel angry. Was this deliberate? Stone seemed set on making her feel ill at east. It wasn't amusing, it was downright rude.

A carpet muffled her steps as she walked. The far end of the corridor was in shadow. She shivered. Despite the slight sounds, the house had a deserted air to it. Reaching out she trailed her fingers along the oak panelling. The feel of the polished wood steadied her.

A door stood open a little way down the corridor, inviting her to enter. A sound reached her, something she couldn't readily identify. Perhaps someone in this room could tell her where Stone was. She pushed at the door and it swung open on well-oiled hinges.

'Excuse me . . .' she began, then stopped, her breath catching in her throat at the sight that met her eyes.

The room was empty except for a few wooden chairs. Stark white walls were cross-hatched by exposed oak beams. The floor of dark polished oak gleamed softly in the light from candles which flickered in iron wall-sconces.

A woman sat facing the door. She wore a device of shiny black straps which left her large breasts bare. A sequinned mask covered her eyes and nose and her glossy black hair was swept high and secured with jet combs. Her legs were spread and across her lap lay another woman, face down and naked except for a broad red belt which was laced tightly around her waist.

Marika gaped in fascination.

The second woman was also masked. Her mask was red, decorated with silver studs. Brown hair was pinned closely to her head, making her head and neck look delicate and vulnerable. She was small and slightly built, the constriction of her waist throwing her rounded buttocks into shocking prominence. She glanced towards Marika and smiled, the tip of her tongue snaking out to wet her red lips.

Marika stood rooted, her eyes drawn to the movement as the seated woman caressed the bare buttocks of the other. After a second or two, she began to spank her gently.

That was the noise Marika had heard. The sound of a palm striking against firm flesh. The taut globes were already rosy, blushing from an earlier spanking. The reddened buttocks seemed to snap against the masked woman's hand as it rose and fell, the sound louder now, crisp in the silence.

Marika wanted to leave, but she couldn't look away. She had never seen anything so dreadful – or so erotic. Each slap as it connected caused a reaction within her, a sort of pulsing wince, as if *she* and not the red-masked woman was being spanked.

Belatedly she began backing out of the

doorway, mumbling an apology. The women ignored her, engrossed in what they were doing. The woman being spanked gave a long, throaty sigh.

There was a movement in the shadows. Only then did Marika notice the other figure in the room.

The man was very tall and slim, dressed entirely in black and with a leather mask covering his upper face and hair. He sat on a wooden settle watching the two women, his hand resting easily on one leather-covered thigh. He looked up and saw Marika.

She saw the glint of dark eyes through the slits in the mask as he grinned. She recognised that strong jawline. Stone.

This was just something else designed to faze her. First the dramatic appearance in the car park and now this. Part of her wanted to march up to him and demand to know what the hell he thought he was playing at. But something stopped her. It was as if a thread connected her to the figure who sat in the shadows, the flickering candlelight sending jagged yellow flashes across his stillness.

When the masked man beckoned to her, she found herself walking into the room as meekly as if this was an everyday event.

'Stone,' she whispered under her breath. He nodded and crooked one elegant finger.

Her legs were shaking. Halfway across the room she stopped. The door stood open behind her, the staircase was within easy reach. No one made a move towards her. Raising her hand she closed her fingers over the pendant. The pearls were smooth, silky to the touch.

She had only to take it off, throw it to the floor at his feet. She could leave now and never come back. Somehow she knew that if she did, it was over.

But she didn't want it to be. All the restlessness of the last few weeks seemed distilled into this one moment. Stone offered so much by his mere presence. He was an enigma, dangerous, threatening to blow her life apart.

She didn't care why she was here. It was enough that she was. Surely it couldn't be mere hours since they'd first met. Little tremors ran up her back. She felt scared, as if she hovered on the brink of an abyss.

Slowly she began to move towards him again. He held out his arms to her. The game was on and she was now a part of it.

The masked man motioned for Marika to kneel in front of him and she did so without a word.

Leaning forward he lifted the pendant and studied it for a second. Then he traced her jawline with one finger.

She saw that he wore a ring on one thumb, almost a replica of the pendant, except that the plain jet oval was adorned with some sort of carving and the pearls surrounding the jet were black. The ring must be priceless.

Marika trembled and hung her head as the masked man ran a fingertip around her mouth, circling and examining her lips. He pushed a finger into her mouth. With a curiously gentle gesture he stoked her head, urging her to suckle. The wooden floor was cold and hard beneath her knees. The toes of her expensive shoes were being crushed and scuffed, but she gave them no thought.

The sound of the spanking continued, loud in the almost empty room. The red-masked woman sighed, a sound of mingled pain and pleasure. Marika ran her tongue around the masked man's finger, all her senses concentrating on his nearness – the feel of his hand on the back of her head; the exciting smell of his leather clothes; the underlying, faint warmth of clean maleness.

Time seemed suspended. She let go of all thoughts, all questions; there was only this moment. He continued to stroke her, cupping the back of her head and moving his fingertips around the indentation at the back of her skull. She was hypnotised by the movement. His finger was warm in her mouth.

The sound of Stone's zip opening brought her up sharp.

Oh yes, God yes, she thought, as he freed his erect cock.

She had never been keen on oral sex, but she had wanted to suck Stone since that first meeting. The firm stem of his penis reared up from the open zip, his pubic curls hidden beneath the leather. He was big and veiny. The moist reddish glans was collared by skin.

Marika smelt the odour of him, salt and musk.

She leaned forward and dabbed at the cock-head with her tongue, lapping up the single thread of clear fluid.

The hand on the back of her head exerted a more insistent pressure. She opened her lips and drew Stone's cock in. The masked man groaned as she ran her tongue around the flaring rim of the glans and then slid the whole length of him into the hot cavern of her mouth.

The women being spanked was moaning

loudly now and the sound found an echo in Marika. Her nipples were so engorged that they pressed painfully against the inside of her lacy bra. The lips of her sex fluttered and pulsed, while her vagina grew wetter and wetter, soaking the crotch of her lace panties.

Marika worked her mouth up and down the masked man's cock-stem, loving the taste and feel of him. The hand on her head directed her movements, taking away her control. She felt the willing submission flood her. How good it was to give herself over to him for a time. She felt oddly safe, as if freed of some great burden.

Stone grasped the base of his cock and worked the skin back and forth as she suckled the swollen end. Marika relaxed her lips and teased the tip with her wet mouth. Stone's moans became frenzied as his climax approached.

The hand in her hair tightened, pulling her own onto him so that her lips butted against the teeth of the open zip. Marika loved the feel of the hard flesh filling her mouth, the vitality and the whole throbbing length of it. She rimmed the bulbous head, sucking strongly at it, tasting the salty fluid of pre-emission.

With a cry he came, his hips jerking in a paroxysm of pleasure. Marika welcomed the full rush of Stone's semen and swallowed it in ready gulps. She held him in her mouth until his erection subsided. When he drew away, she remained kneeling.

Without a word the masked man zipped himself up. He gestured that she was to stand. She did so. Her legs shaking with excitement. All of her seemed concentrated into the throbbing centre between her thighs. She could hardly wait to feel his hands on her.

Marika closed her eyes as Stone reached down to the hem of her dress and began easing it up her thighs with both hands. The fact that she still wore her jacket made his actions even more arousing. It was far more rude than being naked. Soon the silk was bunched around her waist and she felt the warm air of the room on her stockinged thighs.

His hands caressed her legs, slipping over the fine stockings and lingering on the naked flesh above her lace stocking tops. When he dipped a hand between her thighs and ran his thumb over the triangle of lace which imprisoned her pubis, she gasped aloud.

She swayed towards him as he stroked her, dipping the edges of his fingers under the edge of the lace and teasing out the silky brown strands of her pubic hair. His fingertips played over the indentation in the lace which delineated the split in her sex. A tiny moan escaped Marika. The anticipation of his touch on her naked flesh was almost unbearable.

Never had she felt such hunger. Her insides ached with wanting him. The swelling of her sex was almost painful.

With a husky laugh, Stone turned her around and began stroking her lace-covered bottom. Now Marika could see that the women were locked in an embrace. The red-masked one sat on the other's lap, her thighs gaping open while a hand was at work on her. They were kissing passionately.

She saw what she'd missed earlier. Each of the women wore a pendant like hers.

The red-masked woman squirmed as a slippery

finger plunged inside her, and she ground down onto the other woman's knuckles. Marika was poised between fascinated revulsion and arousal. She had never seen two women kissing, let alone masturbating each other. They didn't seem to care that she was staring at them openly.

Stone's hands described gentle circles on her buttocks. She needed something more, something stronger. Burning with an unexpressed need, she arched her back and pressed her bottom towards the masked man.

'Please. Oh please . . .' she gasped.

He laughed softly as his hands squeezed and massaged her, drawing the globes of flesh apart and then allowing them to close. Marika's breath came in hoarse little mewling sounds. Her sex was awash, the whole of it sticky and pliant. She could smell the musky heat of her excitement.

Suddenly she gasped as the masked man slapped her bottom. She squirmed in his grip, but he held her tight, clamping one arm around her waist and tipping her slightly forward. He slapped her again, harder this time. She opened her mouth to protest, but had no chance to cry out as he swung her over his knee, knocking the breath out of her.

Tears of humiliation sprang to her eyes as he spanked her soundly. No one had ever hit her and the burning pain of it was a complete shock. But although she struggled and wept, she was aware of the pressure building inside her. Her sexual tension was actually being increased by the regular contact of his palm against her buttocks.

She had a sudden sharp image of herself, sprawled across him, her linen jacket awry and her expensive silk dress rucked up carelessly above her waist. Long, slim legs flailing helplessly and her lace-covered bottom bobbing and falling under his punishing palm.

She began to groan, the sound forced out between her clenched teeth.

'Oh, God. Oh, God, yes,' she grunted.

He spanked her harder. Each blow landing before the smart of the previous one had faded.

Marika's every nerve end seemed newly alive and sensitized. Her stomach, pressed to his leather-covered thighs, rolled maddeningly against the tactile warmth. She surged against him, hardly conscious that she was thrusting her buttocks at him lewdly, desperate for the next blow of his hand.

The women in the red-mask cried out as she climaxed, her thighs scissoring to trap the other woman's hand inside their silken warmth.

In that same instant Marika's own pleasure peaked. She'd been tipped over the edge by the other women's groans.

She almost screamed at the force of her orgasm. It seemed to sweep her up and leave her stranded in some dark place. She was blind and deaf, her whole body locked into one long tearing ache. The room swam around her. For some moments she had no idea of who she was or what was happening to her.

Gradually she calmed and came back to herself.

She was lying on the oak floor, her dress bunched about her waist and her legs splayed open. One shoe had come off. It lay a few feet away. There was a ladder in one expensive stocking. Her botton burned and throbbed and the crotch of her lace pants was drenched with her milky outpouring.

Marika sobbed for breath. She'd just had the most incredible orgasm and Stone had hardly touched her.

The two women were gone, but the man was sitting on the wooden settle watching her. He said nothing, his dark eyes glittering through the slits in his mask.

As she felt his eyes on her, she curled up with shame. What a spectacle she must look. Her hair had come loose from its ribbon and hung in damp strands around her face. Her make-up must be smudged, the mascara smeared panda-like under her eyes. And he could see the evidence of her arousal in the dark patch between her legs. She'd never seeped like that before.

The feeling of humiliation was crushing. How *could* she have allowed herself to become involved in this perverted little scenario? She threw Stone a pleading glance. He said nothing, only smiled narrowly and beckoned to her.

Suddenly she couldn't meet his eyes. She wanted to leave this place, to retreat to home ground and collect her wits. Struggling to her feet, she pulled down her dress, trying in vain to smooth out the creases in her linen jacket.

The masked man laughed softly, stood up, and took a step towards her. Without a word, he handed her a black card. It was the twin of the one she had found in the box with the pendant. She took the card, glanced at it.

There was a different phone number written in gold lettering.

Puzzled she looked up at him. What was she meant to do with another card? Only then did she realise that he hadn't spoken a single word throughout her ordeal.

'Stone?' she whispered, her voice pleading with him to say something, anything. 'You owe me some sort of an explanation.'

He laughed. It sounded odd. Out of kilter somehow. A suspicion came over her then, something so awful that she could hardly bear to encompass it.

Oh, God no. That couldn't be. But she had to know.

'Take off your mask,' she said, faintly. 'Please. Take it off.'

Slowly the man reached up and detached the mask. As his face came into view Marika shrank inside herself. He was young, blond and good-looking. She had never seen him before.

She gave a strangled cry.

Dear God. She had just fellated and been spanked by a complete stranger. With a moan of horror she fled from the house.

CHAPTER

3

Marika opened her eyes as she heard the key in the lock and then footsteps ascending the stairs.

Half awake, she tensed, the memory of the events of the previous evening surfacing in her mind. Her mouth dried. How stupid to have taken such a risk, to have gone to the address alone. And now what? She could have been followed.

She was on the point of flinging herself out of bed and finding somewhere to hide when James walked breezily into her bedroom, a bunch of roses in one hand and a bottle of Lucozade in the other. Under one arm was a paper.

'My version of tea and sympathy,' he said brightly, throwing the newspaper onto the bed. 'How's the invalid? Awake at last I see. I was worried about you. I've been phoning you since eight this morning.'

Marika sank back with relief, feeling rather foolish for panicking. Of course, he was the only one with a key to the flat besides herself.

James was freshly shaved and smelt of cologne.

His thick dark hair was swept straight back from his forehead, the streaks of silver at his temples adding distinction to his good looks.

She smiled a greeting, his words sinking in slowly. Invalid? For a moment she was puzzled, then she remembered that she'd told him she had a cold.

'I . . . unplugged the phone last night,' she said, emerging from the duvet. 'I haven't been sleeping too well lately.'

Bars of wintery sunlight pushed through the cracks in the figured grey curtains. James grinned as he picked up the bedside clock and turned its face towards her.

'Well it looks like you've made up for lost time.'

It was ten-thirty in the morning. She had slept solidly for the first time in weeks.

'What are you doing here?' she said. 'You always play golf on Saturday mornings.'

'I cancelled. Couldn't bear the thought of you suffering. Looks like I was right to call in.' James glanced around the bedroom.

Clothes and underwear were littered in a straggling line from the en suite bathroom to the bed. He began gathering up garments, dumping some of them in a laundry basket and draping the crumpled linen jacket over the back of a bedroom chair.

Marika coloured as she saw the creased state of the silk dress. It looked as if she'd slept in it. Remembering how it had been rucked up to her waist while her buttocks simmered under the masked man's palm brought her out in a hot sweat.

The pendant lay on the bedside cabinet where she'd put it before slipping into bed and falling asleep almost immediately. While James was occupied, she reached over and slipped it into the drawer of the cabinet.

'Did you find out who sent you that present?' he said with his back to her.

She jumped guiltily. 'Not yet,' she lied. 'I'm sure it was a practical joke.'

'What was in this parcel anyway?' James asked. 'You never said.'

'Or . . . er chocolates,' she improvised. 'I gave them to Gwen. They were probably meant for her anyway. She has her admirers, you know . . .' she trailed off, realising how ridiculous she sounded.

James looked surprised, as well he might, thought Marika. Gwen was built like a scrum half and had a no-nonsense attitude to men. She'd give short shrift to anyone trying to win *her* over with chocolates.

'Well it takes all sorts,' James murmured.

She watched him tidying up, amused by the way he was fussing over her. This solicitude wasn't like him at all.

But then it wasn't like her to be in bed at ten-thirty in the morning. Luckily she didn't have to explain why she had slept in. He seemed satisfied that he'd worked everything out for himself.

She reached for a tissue from the box on the bedside cabinet, having decided that it would be simplest to go along with the lie about having a cold. Sniffing loudly, she put her hand to her throat and winced.

'Sore? Poor baby,' James said. 'Can I get you anything?' He sat on the edge of the bed and patted her hand.

'Mmm. Tea would be nice,' Marika said,

pushing back her tangle of blonde hair and sitting fully upright.

James's blue eyes quickened with interest as the grey, satin covered duvet slipped down to reveal her bare shoulders and the tops of her breasts. She'd fallen into bed the night before, too shattered by her experience to even throw on a nightdress.

Now the cool fabric sliding against her nipples was pleasant and she was more strongly aware of the residual tingling in the flesh of her buttocks as she moved. It was as if she glowed all over with remembered pleasure.

The sudden interest on James's face made her self-conscious.

'You don't normally sleep naked,' he said.

'No. I . . . was hot. I think I had a temperature.'

She was about to ask James to pass her a robe but something stopped her. His blue eyes were intense and she saw the tell-tale bulge in his black jeans.

The flare of sensation at her groin surprised her. Normally she hated sex in the morning. Until she had showered and cleaned her teeth she always felt stale and rumpled and not at all sexy. But something was different today. It was as if a slow red tide was moving within her, rising up and spreading little tendrils of heat along every nerve end.

Under James's appreciative scrutiny she was becoming aroused and it felt good. Already her nipples had hardened. They stuck out like wanton brown cones. She arched her back, lifting her rib cage so that her breasts were thrust into prominence. James gaped at her, his blue eyes clouded with undisguised lust.

'You look different . . .'

'I feel different,' she purred. 'Don't you like me like this?'

She felt sexy, powerful. In fact she hardly recognised herself. Normally James made the first move and she was happy to let him. She found it difficult to reach orgasm, other than when she masturbated, and was content for James to satisfy himself without waiting for her to catch up. At least one of them was happy that way.

She smiled slowly now, holding James's eyes as, deliberately, she let the duvet slip slowly down to her waist. Raising her hands she cupped the full under-swell of her breasts, running her thumbs over her swollen nipples.

James swallowed, his eyes following the movements of her fingers.

'But you're ill. Your cold . . .' he stammered. 'Are you sure this is a good idea?'

Dear James. Always so considerate, even when it was obvious that he was dying to jump on her. The zipper of his black jeans looked about to burst with the pressure behind it. She felt a tiny flicker of irritation. Why didn't he take her in his arms? It wasn't gentleness she wanted now.

She couldn't imagine Stone holding back. The minute the thought popped into her mind she thrust it away. It was unfair to compare the two of them. James was real, warm, caring, and sexy in his own way. Stone was little more than a cipher and from what she had seen of him, he was cold and manipulative.

But somehow he had taken a hold on her, turning her emotions upside down, awakening her to the unexplored shadows within herself.

The thought of Stone sent a new and

treacherous excitement through her. Her sex fluttered and pulsed. She dragged her concentration back to James. This was the man she was fond of, her best friend and lover.

'You needn't kiss me,' she said softly, to James. 'We could do it doggy fashion. That way I'll keep my germs to myself.'

She extricated herself from the duvet and crawled towards him on all fours. Her breasts swung gently as she moved and she rotated her hips in a rolling motion.

James's eyes popped and his hands trembled as he reached for the buttons of his shirt.

'No. Leave it on,' she said. 'I can't wait for you to undress. I want you now.'

Kneeling on the bed, she unfastened the buckle on his belt and undid the zip. Pushing his jeans down to his thighs, she grabbed the waist of his boxers and pulled them down. She looked at his muscular thighs appreciatively. James worked out at a local gym twice a week and had kept his sportsman's physique. There was only a slight thickening around his waist and a little flesh on his pectorals to betray his age.

His erection bobbed into view, jutting up against the bottom edge of his soft cambric shirt. The fabric tented around his shaft and the swollen end peeped out enticingly. He had a nice cock. Long and thick with a pronounced ridge around the glans.

Marika imagined him forcing it into her, holding her down while he rimmed the entrance to her vagina, the ridge pushing deliciously past the initial tightness. But James was far too much of a gentleman to do any such thing and, until now, she had never desired him to.

Reaching for her shoulders James pulled Marika towards him. Kneeling on the bed, facing him, she was on a level with him. His fingers trembled as her blonde hair brushed against his knuckles.

Bending closer he said hoarsely, 'God you're so beautiful.'

Marika controlled her impatience. He was going to kiss her, but she didn't want that. She didn't want him to caress her to readiness either. She didn't need it.

The throbbing between her thighs was insistent and she could feel the wetness gathering. It was incredible. Usually it took a lot of foreplay before she became slippery enough for James to enter her. She'd considered herself to be on the dry side before now.

Something must be happening to her physiography as well as to her libido.

As she pulled out of James's embrace she felt another warm trickle of fluid from her vagina. She shivered slightly in anticipation of being filled by his hard male flesh. All she could think of was the rigid pole that reared up from the tangle of hair at his groin. Couldn't he tell that she just wanted him to screw her?

He made a sound in the back of his throat as she pulled away. His hands reaching for her and clutching only air;.

'No mouths. Germs. Remember?' she said lightly, so as not to offend him.

'Oh . . . yes. Sorry.'

She sensed his confusion and felt a surge of affection for him. Poor guy. It wasn't surprising that he was out of his depth. This was a side of herself that she hadn't known existed. How on earth was he expected to cope with it?

Then she realised that she'd have to show him what she wanted. Shifting position she got up onto all fours again and turned around. Edging towards him, she presented him with a view of her full rounded bottom and the shadowed valley between her cheeks.

She smiled inwardly, imagining the shock and the lust that must be warring on his face. Arching her back, she parted her thighs so that the crevice between her buttocks opened and her sex pouted at him. That ought to be a clear enough signal for him.

James made a strangled noise and mounted her. His cock pressed urgently between her legs. She lifted her buttocks even higher, so that her vagina opened receptively. James moaned as he rubbed the head of his cock up and down her wet folds.

The lips of her sex seemed to flutter around his cock-stem as she pressed back towards him. She felt his pubic hair brush scratchily against her bottom as he worked himself back and forth along her hot, moist channel. Then, as he pushed the head of his cock just inside the entrance to her body, she climaxed.

James moaned as she surged and pulsed around his rigid cock. Losing all control he plunged into her, jamming the swollen head inside her, then drawing almost fully out before slamming back into her.

'God, oh God,' Marika groaned, as wave after wave of pleasure spread right through her.

This was what she'd wanted. She braced herself as James held her around the waist, taking his weight as he lay across her back. She seemed to be having one prolonged climax. The deep, full thrusts of James's cock felt wonderful. Sex had never been so good or so satisfying with him.

When he cried out and came, she used the muscles of her vagina to milk the last drops of semen out of him. James buried his face in her neck, murmuring endearments as they slipped down onto the duvet, still joined together.

For a long time they lay entwined, too exhausted to move. James recovered first. He went to the bathroom to wash himself and reappeared with a warm sponge and towel. Marika washed herself, then got back under the duvet. She smiled up at him.

'I think I'll have that tea now, if the offer's still open.'

He disappeared downstairs and she heard him moving around the kitchen. Soon he reappeared with a tea tray. Setting it on the bed he poured two cups and handed one to Marika.

She sipped, looking at him over the rim of the cup. He hadn't spoken for a time and she saw that he was searching for the right thing to say. She saw also that he was giving her little wary glances every now and then. He was, she realised, extremely unsettled by the way she had taken the sexual initiative.

'You were very different today,' he said finally.

How the English are masters of the understatement, she thought. What could she say? That it was the thought of someone else, someone she'd met briefly in a car park, who'd unlocked some secret place within her? That it was the memory of a masked man spanking her which had made her long for James to plunge into her while his stomach butted against her still sensitised buttocks?

She smiled at the thought of the look that would appear on his face if she were to tell him the truth.

'I felt different. Perhaps there's a touch of spring in the air. I can't explain it. What's the matter? You sound . . .' she sought for the word she wanted, 'disapproving somehow. Didn't you enjoy it?'

'Oh yes. It was fantastic.'

'But . . .?'

'Well it's just that – it didn't seem like you. I've never seen you like that. You were . . . well, almost overwhelming.'

Marika took another sip of the Earl Grey. Oh, it was me all right, James, she said inwardly. A new me, someone I'm only just getting to know. There was a pause while she let the slight atmosphere between them evaporate.

Smiling brightly at him, she said, 'Why don't you phone the golf club? See if you can get a game after all? I feel a lot better now and I've a few things to do today.'

'You're sure?'

'Perfectly. I really don't need you to nursemaid me, though it was very sweet of you to look in.'

He grinned, the lines around his blue eyes crinkling.

'I'm glad I did now. That was quite an experience. You're a dark horse, Marika. I thought I knew you after all this time.'

Again she sensed his unease. He really didn't know what to think. On the one hand he had enjoyed the experience, but on the other he was disconcerted, subconsciously searching for the reason for her sudden outbreak of wantonness.

James kissed her cheek. 'I'll get off then,' he

said, standing up and walking to the door. He glanced at his watch. 'Should be just in time to catch the chaps for lunch.'

'I'll see you on Tuesday, then?'

They had tickets for *Sunset Boulevard*. She was looking forward to it. They shared a love of musicals.

'Shall I pick you up?'

'No. I'll meet you at the Adelphi,' she said. 'I've an early start next day, so I'll bring my car for a quick getaway. That way you can stay and socialise with the others if you want to.'

'OK. Suit yourself.'

At the door he blew her a kiss. She heard his footsteps on the stairs, then the front door slammed behind him.

While Marika showered and washed her hair, she thought over the events of the past few hours; the way she had acted with James and the incredible things which had happened to her in that house.

Even while she resisted admitting to it, she knew that her behaviour this morning had been promoted by her experience at the hands of the masked man. Everything about that episode seemed unreal, as if it had happened to someone else. Except that the remembered pleasure was like something alive, incandescent in her thoughts.

But she didn't want to think about that.

She was furious with Stone. How dare he come bursting into her life, turning everything inside out? He must be some kind of pervert who got his kicks from duping people. And she had fallen for his tricks completely. How gullible he must think her. She felt an utter fool.

Just thinking about the way she'd gone to the address he'd given her made her heart beat faster. I must be mad, completely mad, she thought. It was a stupid, dangerous thing to do. She knew that Stone had planned it all. Lured her to that house under false pretences. He'd wanted her to assume that the masked man was him. But she could find no reason why he would want to humiliate her. He didn't even know her.

If only she could find out who Stone was. Face to face, she could handle him. She imagined the things she'd call him. They weren't pretty.

Opening the drawer of her bedside cabinet, she took out the pendant and the black card with the gold numbers.

The gold chain was cold against her fingers and the oval of jet, enrircled by pearls, looked dense and shiny. She turned it over in her hands, looking for any clue. If she could find out where the pendant came from, she might be able to track down Stone.

But there was no hallmark, no designer's stamp. She turned her attention to the card. It was black and featureless, except for the embossed gold numbers. All she had to do was dial that number. Stone would answer, she just knew it. By now he would know every detail of what had happened in that house.

Well sod him. She wouldn't give him the satisfaction of gloating. Stone could go and take a running jump. She was determined to put him out of her mind.

Slamming the drawer shut, she dressed in loose trousers and a cotton sweater. Downstairs she put on a quilted silk parka and went out of the house.

Walking to the small street market which was ten minutes from her flat, she bought fruit and vegetables. The fresh air brought a glow to her cheeks and she returned home by a circuitous route, to take advantage of the crisp wintery weather.

She made coffee and had a light lunch, then settled down to read through the Collins file. Having begun to get a picture of the client's needs, she sketched an outline of her requirements for a publicity campaign. It was going to be difficult to give a glamourous image to a new line of fake tattoos, but she'd had more difficult products to handle in the past. Soon she had two pages of notes, ready to give to Gwen on Monday.

In the afternoon she watched a Bette Davies film on TV, then it was time to get ready for the book launch.

Marika decided to wear all black. With her creamy skin and natural blonde hair, the colour was dramatic on her. Over a classic Versace dress, she wore a filmy jacket of silk voile sewn with black beads. Black stockings and plain, high-heeled courts completed her outfit.

Her make-up was understated as usual, but she emphasised her mouth with a clear red lipstick. About to leave the bedroom, she hesitated, then opened a drawer. Moved by an impulse she didn't care to think about too deeply, she took out the pendant and slipped it on.

She had a strong hunch that Stone knew all about her movements. The fact ought to have frightened her, but it didn't. It disturbed and intrigued her and it made her angry.

Perhaps he knew that she'd be at Waterstone's

that evening. He might even be there amongst the ageing pop stars and society hangers-on. And if that was the case, he'd see that she was wearing the pendant.

He'd know then that she had taken up his challenge.

The taxi coasted past Regent's Park, taking the outer circle. Despite the pools of light from the college and other buildings it was dark between the trees. Marika glanced out of the window at the joggers who seemed to take no notice of any timetable except their own.

She couldn't imagine what they got out of running in the dark. Settling back she watched night-time London slide past the windows. She didn't feel inclined to chat and was glad that the taxi driver was the strong silent type.

'This do you, love?' the driver said, after pulling into Charing Cross Road and drawing up next to Waterstone's.

'Yes. Thanks.' Marika paid him and got out.

Before going into the shop she looked in Waterstone's window, a small self-congratulatory smile on her lips as she saw the opulence of the display.

The whole of the window was draped with violet silk and Janice Clements's patrician face adorned three large, velvet-backed showcards. Posters for *Elected Her Lover* – an inspired title – were pinned on every available surface and piles of books filled the window. The book jackets were striking – violet, gold and black. A notice advertised that Janice Clements would be signing copies of her book that evening.

Marika opened the door and stepped inside the

shop. She made a point of arriving early for these events. It made the client feel secure when they saw her checking that everything was in place. She located the store manager, exchanged a few words with him, then ran a critical eye over the tables with their arrangements of fresh flowers, stacks of glasses and bottles of champagne.

Everything was perfect. The first guests arrived and she welcomed each of them in turn. Soon the room was thronged with dignitaries, TV personalities, critics and reporters.

Janice Clements arrived with her husband, having timed herself to make a perfect entrance. She was a tall, slim woman in her late forties. Her short dark-brown hair was glossy and expertly styled. The pillar-box red suit she wore was in the new, softer style, without the shoulder pads and strict tailoring of the power dresser. Chunky gold earrings and a single brooch completed her outfit.

Marika smiled her approval. Janice Clements had class and status – the perfect client in fact. As an author she couldn't fail. The publishers were doing everything possible to raise her profile, though it was a well kept secret that Janice herself was paying for much of her publicity and for the lavish party after the signing, which was to be held at the Fifth Floor restaurant at Harvey Nichols.

A ripple of applause greeted Janice's entrance and flash bulbs began popping. Marika steered Janice expertly through the throng and towards the back of the room where various people had begun buying copies of *Elected Her Lover* and were waiting in line to meet her.

The launch and signing went well. Janice spoke a few words to everyone, smiled graciously, and gave interviews for three national newspapers. She chatted at length to the more important guests, and signed around a hundred books. Marika kept to the background, making sure that the evening flowed smoothly. Janice was a pro. She really knew how to 'work a room', as the Americans called it. Marika wished that all of her clients were such experts.

At a given signal Marika announced that the launch was over and gave a small speech, then a fleet of taxis transported the guests to the private party.

At the restaurant, Marika chose to sit at a quiet corner table. Her feet were aching and she wanted to take a breather before she did any more socialising. Sipping a vodka martini, she congratulated herself on a job well done. The pressure was off. Now she could relax and enjoy herself.

She glanced around the restaurant and her eyes met those of a striking young woman. Marika had noticed the woman staring at her earlier, but had not had time to make her acquaintance. She recognised her face from the covers of *Vogue, Elle, Harpers and Queen* and a dozen other glossy magazines.

Having caught Marika's eye, the young woman made her way towards her.

'You've found a quiet corner for yourself. Mind if I join you?' she asked, her voice softly accented.

'Please do,' Marika waved her to the empty seat next to her.

'Thanks. You're Marika Fremen, aren't you? PrimeLight handles some of my modelling friends. You run a tight agency.'

'Thank you. And you're Pia Mason, aren't you?' Marika said coolly. 'Are you a friend of Janice's?'

Marika had drawn up the guest list herself and she knew for certain that Pia's name wasn't on it.

Pia coloured slightly. It was very becoming. Seen close to and even without the benefit of the photographer's air brush, she was strikingly beautiful. Marika felt a stab of unaccustomed envy. Pia's looks – sleek dark hair that lay like wings against her narrow cheeks, olive skin, and the slight tilt to her dark eyes – denoted her Asian origins. Her mouth was full and red, naturally so it seemed.

She wore a short dress of pleated silk chiffon in the new 'little girl' style, her long, well-bred legs looking naked and vulnerable in their pale stockings and high-heeled strappy sandals. Marika thought the current fashion trend hideous, but on Pia it was stunning.

Pia gave an apologetic smile, her eyes tipping up at the corners.

'I'm sort of a gate-crasher. I came along with someone who knows Janice's husband. Do you mind?'

Marika laughed. 'No, I don't mind.'

And it was true. Suddenly she was glad that Pia was there. She felt drawn to the young woman. Attracted by her air of poise that was tempered with natural charm; not something one expected to find in a 'super' model. Most of them were completely self-absorbed.

'Do you like books or is it just parties you enjoy?' Marika asked.

Pia gave her a direct look and there was something unfathomable in her sloping dark eyes.

'It's the people I meet that I find fascinating,' she said. 'You never know who you might run into.'

Was she mistaken, or was there a hidden meaning in those words? Marika sipped her martini, surprised to find that her hand was trembling slightly.

'The old – "A stranger is just a friend you haven't met yet" – syndrome. Is that it?' she said, trying to lighten the atmosphere which had suddenly become strangely intense. Pia reminded her of someone, but she couldn't recall who.

Pia smiled, her full red mouth curving sweetly. 'Something like that.'

She really is lovely, Marika thought again; she must have lots of admirers. She glanced away at the crowded room, watching light winking off expensive jewellery, but her eyes were drawn back to Pia's face. She was surprised at herself. Usually she didn't dwell too much on other women's looks.

Pia didn't seem to mind being looked at. Probably she was used to it. She leaned forward now and her eyes glittered.

Lowering her voice she said, 'I have to talk to you – alone. We have something in common.'

Marika's pulses quickened. Somehow she had known. Pia had not come to Janice Clements's party on a whim. Her throat was dry when she answered.

'What . . . what do you mean?'

'I think you know,' Pia said, dipping her hand inside the high neckline of her little girl dress.

Marika watched with horrified fascination as Pia drew a gold chain free, her hand cupping whatever it was that was suspended there. But Marika knew already. Even before Pia opened her palm and she saw the pendant of jet surrounded by pearls.

A wave of heat washed over her and she felt faint for a moment. Now she knew who Pia reminded her of. Not in looks, but in a certain detachment of manner, a knowingness about her dark eyes that had nothing to do with age or gender.

'Do you need to stay here?' Pia said.

'What? . . . Er no, not really. I've finished now. This is the pleasure part of things for me.'

Pia stood up and held out her hand.

'Then let's get out of here, shall we? We can go to my house. There's a lot we have to talk about.'

Marika took Pia's hand, feeling the slim fingers curl around her own. It didn't occur to her to refuse. Pia was about to supply part of the puzzle and she couldn't wait to hear what she had to say.

CHAPTER

4

Pia lived in a narrow-fronted Georgian house in a mews off Cadogan Square. Bay trees in wooden tubs stood either side of the red front door.

'Come in. The sitting-room's through there. I'll make coffee,' she said, closing the front door behind Marika.

Marika followed her into the kitchen.

'Can we chat while you make the coffee?' she said.

Pia smiled. 'Of course.'

The kitchen was white and gleaming. Marble work tops covered their expensive units and white, slatted-wood blinds hung at the picture windows.

Pia spooned beans into a coffee grinder, then placed the ground coffee into a cafetiere. The dark brown smell of coffee filled the kitchen.

Marika broke the silence. 'What do you know about a man called Stone?'

Pia's look of surprise seemed genuine.

'Who? That's a fanciful name. Or is it a surname?'

'You really don't know him? But . . . I thought – the pendant . . . Isn't that why you brought me here? What *is* going on?'

'You have no idea at all, have you? Sit down,' Pia said, putting a cool, comforting hand on Marika's arm. 'I see that we've really got a lot to talk about.'

She poured coffee and handed a cup to Marika. Lifting her hands to her neck she took off her pendant and laid it on the table between them. Marika saw at once that Pia's pendant differed from her own. The oval of black jet was carved with the design of a heart.

'I think you'd better explain,' Marika said. 'How did you come by this pendant?'

'It was given to me some time ago. I was on a fashion shoot in Milan. Someone put it in my hotel room. I never found out who. There was a card with it.'

Marika nodded. 'Black with gold lettering?'

'Yes. They're always the same.'

'And you phoned the number on the card?'

Pia's eyes held hers; they did not waver. 'Of course. But you knew that much, didn't you?' Her voice was soft. 'And that was the start of everything. I found a new dimension to my life. You know something about that also or you wouldn't be here now.'

Marika didn't reply. It was far too soon to divulge anything to this young woman. She liked her, but she didn't trust her yet. She waited for Pia to continue.

'I've found certain things out, or rather they've been told to me over a period of time. I'm – we – are part of an exclusive society. It has a name. The Discipline of Pearls. Members are recruited by the 'elders' – people who founded the society. The term 'elder' is a title. It doesn't denote age, but it carries the distinction of rank. Prospective members are investigated and screened by the elders before being approached, then they are presented with a pendant and a black card. The rest is up to the individual. They have freedom of choice. There is no pressure for anyone to enter the society's ranks.'

Marika digested the information. It was a shock to find out that her experience was not unique. The Discipline of Pearls. It sounded exotic. She had never dreamed that there might be an organised body involved. Her thoughts had been centred on Stone. But Pia appeared never to have heard of him.

She wanted to know more. It was hard to believe that Pia could have experienced anything like she had. Taking a sip of her coffee, she let a small space of time elapse.

'What happened when you telephoned the number on the black card?' she asked Pia bluntly.

Pia coloured slightly, her olive skin taking on a peach tinge, but she didn't try to avoid the question.

'I was told to go to an address, a crumbling villa on the outskirts of Milan. I tried to ask questions, but the woman I spoke to was not forthcoming. She said I had a choice. If I went I must do exactly as I was told. Otherwise I could throw away the card and carry on my life, unchanged. It was like a challenge, you understand? I had to see what I would find.'

Marika understood. She had responded to the same impetus.

'It was night and the villa was empty, lit only by

moonlight,' Pia said. 'It was hot. There was a fountain playing, in a tiled courtyard. A flight of deep stone steps led up to a balcony and a grape vine was entwined in the stone balustrade. It was so beautiful, like something out of *Romeo and Juliet*.'

Pia's eyes glazed over as she remembered. Her red mouth looked soft and childlike. As she spoke, Marika could almost see the villa with its marble pillars and ancient tiled floor.

'I sat on the wide stone lip of the basin, listening to the cascading water. The stone was cool against my skin. I wore only a thin, white summer dress. Underneath I was naked. That was part of my instructions. I lifted the skirt so that I could feel the roughness of the stone against my bare skin. I thought I was alone, but a man stepped out of the shadows. He beckoned to me and, after a moment, I went to him.'

She paused and glanced at Marika. 'I could have walked away at any time – I was very clear about that – but I didn't. I did exactly as he told me to. When he asked me to, I tore off my dress and I held my wrists out to him, so that he could tie them. I saw that he wasn't young, but he was strong and still handsome. When he smiled his teeth were very white. He lifted me and sat me on one of the wide stone steps, then he secured my hands to an iron ring set in the wall above me.'

Marika listened, her excitement mounting. There were similarities in their experiences. Pia continued, her voice even and expressionless.

'He told me to spread my legs and I did so. The pressure on my arms forced me to sit up straight. I knew that my ribs were stretched and my breasts were jutting straight out. The sweat rolled down my skin. I felt it pool in the grooves on either side of my belly.

'For a while he just looked at me and I seemed to feel his eyes on my skin. Then he ran his hands all over me, my shoulders, breasts, belly, the insides of my thighs. I almost died with the shame of it. What was worse was that I *wanted* him to do those things. He put his fingers in my mouth, examining me as if I were a prize animal, feeling my hair, smelling my skin, then he knelt before me and spread my thighs so wide that I thought my bones would crack. When he began licking me I screamed. I couldn't help it. With one hand he held the lips of my sex open. He plunged his tongue inside me, while he dug his thumbs into the flesh of my buttocks.'

Again, she paused. And the tip of her tongue came out to moisten her full red lips.

'I twisted and turned, arching my back and pulling against my wrist bonds, but he didn't stop. He licked and sucked at my pussy, while at the same time his fingers poked crudely into my body, stretching my anus and hurting me. But I welcomed the hurt. I thought I would dissolve with pleasure. I sobbed as I came. I remember that the pleasure seemed to go on for a long time. And when I thought it had finished, he pushed his thick cock into me and rode me hard, squeezing my breasts in his big strong hands. I came again, and again, screaming and crying out, but no one heard me. After he'd finished with me, he untied my wrists and left me. I put on my dress and found my way back to the hotel.'

There was silence when Pia had finished speaking. Marika found that she was breathless and there was a tight, hard knot in her stomach.

'Weren't you terrified?' she asked, when she could speak.

'Yes, of course. But it was also the most exciting thing that had ever happened to me. I knew somehow that I wasn't in actual danger. There was always the feeling that I could have walked away, but I didn't want to. Not ever again, not after that first time.'

'There have been other occasions – like that?'

'Many of them. But each time it's different. I never know what to expect – that's what makes the secret society so compelling. And you have the same choices as me now. All you have to do is make contact each time. After that, what happens is out of your hands. It will be a little easier for you, because I have explained how all this works. I had to find everything out for myself.'

Pia looked unsure of herself for the first time since they'd entered her house.

'One thing. You must swear never to tell anyone that you've spoken to me about the Discipline of Pearls. There are only two rules, but they are strictly adhered to. Once you have accepted the gift of membership you must observe absolute secrecy and absolute obedience. You have not fully accepted membership yet, so I shouldn't be telling you all this.'

'In that case, you've put yourself at risk by speaking to me at all. Why did you do so?'

Pia smiled and shrugged. 'I don't know. A whim? I liked the look of you. You appear so cool and calm, so much in control. I watched you tonight, the way you handled people. You get just so close, then you pull back. But there's something about you, something that speaks of hidden passions. I wondered whether it was that which made one of the elders approach you. And you are defiant. You wore the pendant for all to see it. No one but an innocent would do that. By the way, how did you receive your pendant?'

Marika told her. Pia blew a silent whistle.

'That's very unusual. They are usually sent, not delivered. Sounds like someone has something special planned for you.'

She sounded envious for a moment. 'So this is the man you asked me about? Stone? Clearly he made quite an impression on you.'

'Yes, he did. Do you think he might be one of the elders?'

'It's possible. There's only one way to find out.'

Marika knew what that was. She nodded.

'Phone the number on the card.'

Before she left Pia's house, having exchanged phone numbers with her, she asked her about something else which had been bothering her.

'You say that the elders investigate new members. How much do they know about me?'

'Everything. Their methods are thorough. But don't worry, the paramount rule is that members make all the running. No one will ever bother you. If you choose not to use the telephone number, you'll never hear from them again. I know what's bothering you. You think they'll invade your privacy, come to your house? It won't happen. Look at my pendant. See the inscription? I've been a member of the society for two years now. Never in all that time has anyone approached me.'

Marika smiled, feeling somewhat reassured. She put on her faille evening coat, ready to go out to the taxi which Pia had telephoned for her.

As the taxi drove back towards Regent's Park,

she thought of one thing. Pia had spoken of rules, strict measures to ensure the security of the members of the secret society. But Pia had broken those rules herself, by speaking to Marika.

And Stone had stepped out of character too. She couldn't begin to understand the implications of those two separate things.

One thing she did know: she was going to phone the number on that black card and demand to know why Stone had chosen to bestow the gift of the pendant – and the Discipline of Pearls – on her.

It took Marika two days to get up the courage to pick up the phone.

At the office Gwen commented on how edgy she seemed. It was true. She didn't seem to be able to concentrate on anything. Somehow she got through Monday, leaving Gwen to deal with the bulk of her work. Gwen was capable and efficient, passing on various documents for signature and placing memos in the in-tray, but leaving Marika very much to herself.

Marika chewed on the end of a pen and stared out at the grey sky outside the office window. It wasn't like her to be so indecisive. She was used to making decisions for other people; now it seemed that she couldn't do the same thing for herself.

She drank far too much black coffee and by the time she left the office had a blinding headache. Back home, she collapsed exhausted onto the bed and slept as if she was drugged.

On Tuesday night she sat through *Sunset Boulevard* with James, hardly able to take in any of the performance. In the theatre bar afterwards, she made conversation, sipped a Perrier with lemon, and appeared to James and their mutual friends to be relaxed. But in reality she wasn't there at all. She was thinking about Pia and her experience in Italy.

How would it feel to have a man pleasure her in that way? She could imagine the roughness of the cold stone against her skin, the ropes around her wrists, and the hot silkiness of the stranger's tongue as he plunged it into her body.

The thought of being bound excited Marika madly. It was as if, by tying her wrists, the man had compelled Pia to becomed centred on her own pleasure, a pleasure to which *he* was subject. For it was only after Pia had climaxed that he pushed his cock into her and eased his own tension.

Pia had had many subsequent encounters, each of them as erotic and challenging as that first time.

Is that what she could expect if she accepted the invitation to join the society? Marika had already experienced one mind-blowing sexual encounter. And the memory of it was eating away at her, disturbing her equilibrium.

She wanted more of the same – she wanted to thrust the whole thing from her mind – oh God, she wished she knew what was happening to her.

She had to find out more about Stone, because to her, everything centred around him. She was honest enough to admit to the fact that it was him she wanted to meet in some secluded place – his hands she wanted on her – his mouth . . .

She could see him so clearly. The lean face with high cheekbones, his dark hair close-cropped so that it hugged his skull. And his eyes, dark and calm, with that implacable look of self-possession in them.

'Marika? Hey, are you with us?' One of her friends laughed.

'Oh, sorry. I was thinking about work,' she said.

James slipped his arm around her waist.

'Isn't that typical? You work too hard, love. What you need is a holiday.'

She smiled. 'You could be right. Maybe we should arrange something.'

Perhaps she did need to get away and take stock of herself. She had been happy, settled, a few short weeks ago. Now she was a bundle of nerves, not at all sure what she wanted from life.

She leaned against James. He felt solid, dependable and she knew that he was there for her, within the restrictions they had set themselves. So why didn't that make her feel better? Once he had been enough for her. It wasn't him who had changed.

The restlessness inside her was almost tangible. She imagined it as a seed, growing and spreading tangled, whippy branches right through her.

She took a big swallow of the mineral water, coughing when the bubbles fizzed up her nose. Everyone laughed. She laughed too, but there was an ache in her throat.

There was a solution to the problem, if only she could reach out for it. Why was she trying to deny it? Suddenly she was sick of fighting herself.

Although she had half-expected to hear it, Stone's voice was still a shock.

'Ah, Marika. I've been expecting you.' The silky tones sent a shiver down her back. 'Can I assume that your first assignation was satisfactory?'

'Let's stop playing games shall we, you slippery bastard,' she said coldly. 'You tricked me. Who are you and what do you want from me?'

'Who's playing games, me or you?' he said, sounding amused. 'You could have left that house, but you chose to stay. And I know that you've been speaking to Pia. So you must know all about the secret society. It was remiss of Pia to contact you, but I'll see that she is dealt with gently. I can understand why she was drawn to you.'

Marika was taken aback. How could he know about Pia? Unless he was having her watched or Pia told him herself. She remembered that Pia had broken the rules of secrecy by approaching her.

'You won't harm Pia, will you?' she said, suddenly afraid for the young woman.

Stone laughed softly. 'Our intention is to harm no one, to do nothing, in fact, unless one of our members seeks us out. Haven't you realised that yet?'

'I don't know what to think,' she snapped. 'You talk in riddles and avoid answering direct questions. I don't understand why I've been chosen. I didn't ask for this. Why won't you just tell me what you want?'

His voice deepened, became husky.

'I? This is not a personal matter, though I am flattered that you think so. The Discipline of Pearls offers you possibilities. The issue, Marika, is what do *you* want? I think you are already beginning to find that out. Ask yourself why you phoned this number. You were not forced to.'

She was silent for a moment, digesting his words. He seemed determined to give nothing about himself away.

'I don't believe that you are as dispassionate as you pretend,' she said evenly. 'Why did you deliver the pendant personally? Pia said they are usually sent.'

'It is unusual, but not unknown for one of us to make the initial contact. You are a special case. You have great potential, Marika.'

'Potential for what?'

She heard the smile in his voice as he deliberately avoided answering directly.

'We need people like you in our society. People who are prepared to take risks, to step outside of their everyday personas. Now – no more questions. I believe that we only discover the truth about ourselves through experience. If you choose to become one of our number, go to this address . . .'

It was a hotel this time. She knew it well, having used it to put up clients when they had to be at television studios early in the morning. It was in Kensington, a luxurious and expensive building, and as impersonal as most large hotels are.

There was a silence on the line. As before, she sensed that Stone was going to hang up.

'Will you be there . . . this time?' she asked quickly. Then bit her lip, regretting her show of interest.

'Do you want me to be?' he said softly. 'It can happen.'

God damn the man. He seemed totally incapable of giving a straight answer. Her temper rose and she let it grow. She felt good when she was angry.

'And what if I decide not to go to that hotel?' she said. 'I could tear up this card and forget that I ever met you.'

She waited for his reply, expecting him to reason with her.

'That's up to you, Marika. You know the rules now. You can just walk away from this. But I don't believe that you will. I think you're the type of woman who likes to see things through. When you get to the hotel, go to reception. They'll be expecting you.'

He rang off.

Marika replaced the receiver slowly. Stone was very sure that she'd follow his instructions. She'd love to surprise him and do as she'd threatened. But she knew that he was right. She couldn't just walk away.

Hurrying upstairs she opened the drawer of her bedside cabinet and took out the pendant. The weight of it, the coldness of the gold chain against her palm, felt familiar now.

Lifting her hands she slipped the chain over her head.

CHAPTER

5

Marika stepped out of the swing doors of the hotel and emerged into the foyer.

Marble steps led towards a reception desk, art deco in design, which had spot lamps shining down onto its polished chrome and black marble panels.

Walking past the glass cases which held displays of expensive jewellery and designer evening clothes, she glanced to one side, where the foyer opened out into a lounge. Smartly dressed guests sat on sofas upholstered in cream and black leather, drinking coffee and reading magazines.

Marika's gaze swept over the various guests. Was she here to meet one of those people? Perhaps someone was watching her, waiting for her to give her name. She had no idea what to expect. The only thing she *was* certain about was that Stone was completely unpredictable.

Her mouth was dry, but she gave no outward sign of nervousness. One or two men looked towards her. One of them, an elderly man wearing impeccably tailored clothes, smiled appreciatively and her heart gave a lurch. His cool grey eyes swept over her, taking in the tan suede skirt-suit which she wore over a cream linen blouse.

Was this her contact? She slowed down, giving him the chance to approach her, but he made no move towards her. Instead a set look came over his face and he hid behind a newspaper. She flushed. Oh God, he thinks I'm a tart looking for custom, she thought.

How stupid of her to make such a mistake. For just a moment she felt exposed, imagining that all eyes were on her. But she knew she was being irrational. She told herself that these people were strangers, all of them wearing the blank disinterested look of hotel guests everywhere. Each of them was locked into a separate, private life.

Recovering her poise, she started forward and stopped in front of the desk.

'My name is Marika Fremen,' she said to the young man with the helpful smile. 'I believe I am expected.'

The young man pushed a few buttons on a keyboard and scanned a computer terminal.

'Ah, yes, madam. A reservation has been made for you. If you would just register.'

Marika signed the print-out and handed it to him. The young man handed her the piece of plastic which served as a door key.

'Room two four two, on the second floor. Do you need any help with your luggage?'

'No. Thank you. Oh, one other thing. Would you tell me who made the reservation?'

The young man consulted the computer again.

'The reservation was made in your name and the account settled in cash,' he said. 'No other name was given.'

Marika raised her eyebrows, but said nothing.

'Is there a problem, madam?'

'No. No problem.'

'Then I hope you enjoy your stay.'

She smiled her thanks and made her way towards the lifts. Outside her room, Marika placed the plastic card in the slot and pulled it downwards. The door opened silently onto a plush, executive-class room.

A marble-lined bathroom led off to the left and a mirror-covered wardrobe faced it. The bedroom was decorated in black and cream. Wall lights of chrome and pink glass spread a soft glow over the king-size bed and stylish fittings. Heavy cream drapes hung at the floor-length window.

Marika's eyes were drawn immediately to the slim, square box which lay on the centre of the cream bedcover. There was an envelope on top of the box. Throwing her suede jacket onto a chair, she reached for the envelope and tore it open.

A single sheet of paper was inside. She saw at once that the note was unsigned. As she scanned the neatly typed words, she felt the colour climb into her cheeks.

'Make yourself comfortable,' she read. 'A meal has been ordered for you. Please bathe and put on the clothes in the box. At precisely ten p.m. you will kneel, facing the bed and with your back to the door. Someone will enter the room. On no account are you to look around.'

She read the message twice, her brain churning with questions. Had Stone written that note? She had half a mind to screw up the piece of paper and storm out of the hotel, but she knew that she wanted to see this through. Staring down at the box, she weighed the composition of her emotions.

Uppermost was rebellion. It was contrary to her nature to follow orders. But she was also aware of a hot little core of sexual tension. A pulse was throbbing somewhere deep within her, like a tiny scarlet heartbeat.

Lifting the lid off the black cardboard box, she discovered that it was packed with white tissue paper. Underneath she found a folded garment of black leather. As she took it out and held it up, she drew in her breath.

The halter-necked body was made of the softest kid leather and lined with red silk. The zipped front, collar and revers, and strategically placed zips gave it a 'biker girl' look.

It was a garment meant to be worn purely for sex. There was a racy, tarty look to it that Marika found compelling. Anyone wearing something like that was saying 'look at me, look how sexy I am'. It was not the sort of thing she'd ever think of buying for herself, but the thought of wearing it, feeling the silky lining against her skin, made her excited.

She imagined how it would feel to be zipped tightly into the garment, to have the narrow crotch pressing against her sex. Just the thought of that made her tingle and burn. Bringing the body to her face, she breathed in the enticing smell of new leather.

She glanced once more at the single sheet of paper, which lay discarded on the bed. The certainty that whatever was going to happen would be with her full consent settled gradually over her. And with that decision made, she experienced a sense of fatality. Membership of the

Discipline of Pearls was something she not only wanted – she needed it, even craved it.

Somehow the elders of the society had perceived the emptiness in her life and sent Stone to recruit her to their number. Membership of the society would add a new dimension to her life. Deep down she knew that the die had been cast when she picked up the phone that first time and spoke to Stone.

It was now eight p.m. She had two hours to kill before her mysterious visitor arrived. She stepped into the bathroom and ran a bath.

Scented steam filled the small, tiled room. Marika lay back and let the hot foamy water slide over her skin. Closing her eyes she ran her fingers over her wet skin, feeling the dips and hollows of her neat waist and flaring hips. She knew she was in good shape. The leather body would look good on her.

While she was wrapped in a towel, drying herself, there was a tap at the door and the meal was delivered.

Too hyped up to eat very much, she picked at the salad of hearts of palm and asparagus and nibbled at a small piece of spicy chicken. After applying fresh perfume, she picked up the leather body and put it on. The silk clung to her warm damp skin as she stepped into the garment and smoothed it over her hips.

The leather fitted her snugly. In fact the garment seemed designed specifically to make the wearer focus her awareness on her most sensitive body parts. Her cleavage pressed upwards towards the V-shaped low neck, her breasts compressed and held captive by the shaped bodice.

Zips curved across the fullest part of her breasts and stretched from the centre back of the garment, right underneath her crotch and back up to her belly. A strap buckled tightly around her waist.

Marika's shoulders and back were bare, the fact seeming to underline the constriction of her covered body parts. The feeling was strange, but not unpleasant. The very opposite in fact. She admired her reflection in the mirrored wardrobe. Her blonde hair and fair skin looked stark in contrast to the shiny black leather.

How naked her arms and legs looked. Almost vulnerable, and very appealing.

As ten p.m. approached she began to get nervous. Her earlier bravado was fading fast. It's only the fear of the unknown, she told herself; Stone and Pia had assured her that no harm would come to her and she believed them.

But until now she had been a woman in control of her life – perhaps too much in control. The idea of following anyone's orders did not sit easy with her.

She realised suddenly that, by agreeing not to look around at whoever came into the room, she would be performing an act of faith. Perhaps this was a test, some sort of initiation. It must be vital that the members of the secret society trust each other, otherwise the whole thing would fall apart.

How long had the Discipline of Pearls been in existence? She would ask Pia, next time they met.

Then she heard something. A footfall outside her room. Surely it was too early, barely five minutes to the hour. Her heart beating fast, she hurried to the side of the bed and knelt down. Steeling herself to remain in position she concentrated on the feel of the plush carpet under her knees, the shadowed folds in the thick cream window drapes.

Her ears strained for the tiny sound of the card in the lock, but nothing happened. She thought that she must have been mistaken and began to get up, when the door opened and someone stepped into the room.

Marika froze, halfway to her feet, unable to control the sudden trembling of her limbs. Whoever had walked into the room had stopped. She heard the sound of an indrawn breath. A murmur of appreciation.

'You look enchanting in that outfit, as I knew you would. But did you not read *all* of the instructions?'

It was a man's voice. Marika was certain that it *was* Stone this time. There was no mistaking the dry humour, the even tone. She dared not turn around to see if she was right. But she didn't need to see his face. His features were imprinted on her memory, as indelibly as a tattoo on skin.

A little rush of exaltation seemed to race into every part of her. He's here, she thought, he came here for me. She sensed that it was unusual for him to arrange a liaison. Was this akin to breaking cover?

'I'm waiting,' he said, his voice low and husky, perfectly controlled. 'You know what it required of you. In ten seconds I'm going to leave this room and not come back. If you don't wish to participate, you can hand me your pendant. You'll never hear from me again.'

The silence between them was tangible. Slowly Marika sank to her knees. Her pulses were racing. The thought of him leaving was too awful to contemplate. She didn't care that he wished to remain unseen. It was a kind of triumph to have him there at all.

Her knees sank into the carpet and she felt the silken coolness of the bed-cover as it brushed against her thighs. The hand on the back of her neck made her gasp. She felt him sweep the heavy fall of her hair over one shoulder. Strong hands smoothed along the undersides of her arms, exerting pressure so that she leaned forward against the quilted satin, her arms stretching out in front of her.

She clenched her hands. His message was clear. She was to remain in that position and not touch him – or herself. The restriction sent a little shudder through her. How like him to find the very thing that would push her to the limit of pleasure.

At his touch, at the smell of his hair and skin as he bent over her, she felt a surge of pure lust, almost unbearable in its intensity. Her clitoris pulsed and throbbed, the pressure of the tight leather that imprisoned her swollen sex a torture to her.

Stone laughed, softly.

He knows, she thought. He's absolutely in tune with me. She didn't try to reason it out. It seemed impossible that this man who she hardly knew could be so knowledgeable, so attuned to her hidden sensuality, when James was hardly aware of it at all.

Stone stroked up the sides of her body, his fingers trailing over the zips and massaging the flesh of her breasts. The cold teeth of the zips rubbed against her nipples, chafing them to hard, tactile peaks. They jutted against the shiny fabric with hurting pressure.

She felt Stone's breath on her neck, and then for the briefest of time, the hot touch of his lips on her skin. Oh God, I can't stand it, she thought. He's hardly touched me and I'm about to come. Her hips jerked involuntarily as he bent over her, the hardness of his erection pressing solidly up against the groove of her buttocks.

Marika laid her cheek against the satin of the bedcover, her eyes squeezed tight, as Stone bit gently at her neck. Little shivers of pleasure rippled over her skin. The moan fought its way into her throat, but she caged it behind her teeth.

'So beautiful,' Stone breathed. 'So full of fire, yet willing to submit. And so wonderfully receptive.'

She longed to turn around, to feel his lips on her mouth, but she understood that her pleasure would be heightened by her self-restraint and by what he denied her. Stone moved away for a moment and she made a tiny sound of distress.

He lifted a scrap of material over her head and positioned it around her eyes. It took all of Marika's will power to keep still. This was something she hadn't expected and she felt new rebellion rising within her. Her hands jerked against the coverlet.

Stone paused as if gauging her reactions. Satisfied when she sank down and made no complaint, he tightened the black silk scarf around her eyes. Marika relaxed against him completely. After all, the blindfold was only a symbol of her willingness to play her part in the scenario he had instigated.

As she rubbed her cheek against the bed-cover, her hair spilled around the black scarf, tumbling in a soft plume into the cream satin.

'Perfection,' Stone breathed. 'Black against blonde. You should wear black leather more often.'

His fingers stroked her naked back, massaging the small knobs of her spine. She let her weight rest against the softness of the enormous bed as he caressed her gently and expertly.

His touch was mesmeric, adding a new dimension to the erotic tension on which her whole concentration was centred. It was if she trembled on the edge of an abyss. If she fell she would be shattered by explosions of pleasure, but Stone kept her teetering, wanting, thirsting.

His hands cupped the leather-covered globes of her buttocks, squeezing, lifting and rolling them. The sensation of the silk sliding against her skin was maddening. The crotch was wet with her juices and rubbed against her swollen folds as Stone stroked and plucked at the leather body.

Reaching around her, he pulled gently on the zipper fastenings that bisected the fitted bodice. Marika bit her lips as the leather parted slowly and her constricted breasts burst free, her aching nipples scraping past the cold metal teeth.

Oh God, she must look like some cheap centrefold with her breasts hanging down, forced into elongated ovals; her upturned bottom, full and heart-shaped, the pale globes bisected by the narrow band of shiny black leather. But, through the dawning shame, she knew that she loved that image of herself, so sexy and wanton and such a contrast to her usual uptight persona.

I'm my own alter ego, she thought, trembling with a lust that was bone-deep and still mounting. It was a heady discovery.

Stone's fingers plucked at her flesh, rolling her

nipples between finger and thumb, pulling them into little tubes of tingling pleasure.

'So prominent. Beautiful,' he murmured. 'More than I'd hoped for.'

Marika buried her head in the coverlet, muffling her groans as he kneaded the hanging weight of her breasts. Her face burned with mortification. Thank God he couldn't see her expression. As he continued to pinch and squeeze, she writhed against him, squeezing her thighs together to try to ease the pounding heat of her groin.

She squeezed her eyes shut. Behind the mask it should have been black. But it was scarlet, a deep pulsing red.

Stone laughed softly. 'What a flower of passion you are. Shall I relieve you now?'

'Yes. Please. Oh, please,' she found herself whispering.

'I can't hear you,' he said.

'Do it to me. Oh God . . . Just do it. Please . . .'

She'd never begged before, but she'd never wanted to feel a man inside her so much. She ached for the feel of his rounded glans opening her, sliding into her, the thick shaft filling her. That was all that mattered.

She seemed to be dissolving into sensation. Her sex was awash. Losing the last of her inhibitions, she began to plead with him.

'Hush, my darling,' Stone murmured, though there was no gentleness in his voice, just a measured control. 'In my own time.'

One hand slipped inside the silk-lined gusset and cupped the plum of her sex protectively, while he reached for the zipper at the small of her back and pulled it down. With a tearing sound the taut leather parted and slipped partway across the cheeks of her buttocks. Now she was bisected by a black strip, the crotch split and pulled apart. Stone removed his hand and Marika's soaking sex bulged through the toothed gap.

It seemed the final insult. She was displayed fully for his pleasure now, bulging at breast and buttocks, and unable to hide the shiny red folds of her sex.

Stone used two fingers to rub her, massaging her clit with a slow insulting rhythm that made her weep with shame. Burrowing her head in the coverlet, she arched her back, unable to stop herself from thrusting her buttocks towards his caressing hand.

When he pushed his fingers into her, curving them so that he stroked the sensitive pad behind her clitoris, she bucked and cried out.

'That's it, Marika. Reach for it,' Stone whispered. 'Isn't it wonderful to find your true self? I knew you'd be like this . . .'

While he was speaking, he freed his cock and slipped on a condom. She felt its rubber-covered length pressing against the naked and parted groove of her buttocks, the column of it hot and throbbing and velvet smooth. Holding her breath, she willed him to enter her. He placed one hand on the small of her back and pressed her more closely down onto the bed-cover, while his other hand pressed her thighs more widely apart.

She whimpered, almost beside herself with wanting as her buttocks gaped obscenely. How horrifying it was to know that he could see everything: the damp furrow, the creased brown rose of her anus, and below that her pouting, weeping vagina.

Sliding up and down her yearning crevice, Stone smoothed her juices over the head of his covered cock. Marika grunted and parted her thighs, straining towards him as she felt the big blunt glans pressing her open and forcing a pathway inside her.

Her flesh welcomed him, pulsing and twitching as he crammed himself into her, pubic hair grazing her wide-spread valley. It seemed that she discovered new sensations inside her. Never had her tight passage been plundered so deeply.

She came at once as he pounded into her, gasping and crying out. The flickers of pleasure didn't fade, they settled into a sort of continued internal sensitivity. Every stroke, every contact of his shaft against her lubricated inner walls, brought her gasping and crying towards new levels of pleasure.

Oh, Christ. Is this what multi-orgasmic is? she thought dimly, through the haze of bliss.

Stone bent over her, his arms braced besides hers on the cream coverlet. The pressure of his hands made indentations in the bed and her hands slipped down towards his. As he began thrusting hard and fast, she edged one hand towards his until she touched him. Lifting her little finger, she covered his own.

With her fingertip she caressed the heavy ring he wore, knowing that it would be an oval of jet encircled by black pearls. Stone interlocked his fingers with hers, and it was that gesture, and the knowledge of the tiny intimacy so close to her sightless face, which urged her to her final and most shattering climax.

Opening her mouth against the bedcover, Marika screamed her release, feeling the muffled sound vibrate through her chest. Stone cried out and rose up against her, the head of his cock nudging against her spasming womb as he climaxed.

For one crystalline moment, they seemed joined on all levels, their pulsating flesh an echo of a deeper, more ancient bond.

It was a few moments before either of them moved. Their fingers remained enmeshed, Stone holding onto Marika with a grip like iron. Then he came back to himself. He seemed to realise what he was doing and let go of her hand, then he withdrew from her body, and pushed himself away from her.

Marika had collapsed onto the bed, her upper body sprawled across the coverlet and her hips and legs trailing across the plush carpet. She stayed where she was, waiting for Stone to untie the silk scarf and take her in his arms.

She was certain that he would. For, whatever he had intended, they had shared an experience of rare intimacy. She knew that she was changed for ever and he was affected too. Her lips curved in a small smile of triumph. That wasn't just a fuck, Stone, whatever you might think.

'Stay there for a moment. I want to look at you,' he said.

And she was happy to comply. She didn't think she could move yet, not even if the hotel caught fire.

She heard him moving about, dressing, then she felt him put one hand on the bed. The mattress dipped as he sat down.

'No. Don't move,' he said, when she stirred and turned blindly towards him. 'Stay as you are. That's how it has to be. It's part of the game.'

She understood, though disappointment swept over her in a crushing wave. He wanted to hold her, she knew that he did. Perhaps tenderness was the constraint he put on himself.

'Is it always like this?' she whispered.

There was a moment of silence. She wished that she could see his face, read his expression. Then, she felt his hand stroking her hair, smoothing it back from her damp forehead. She nuzzled his hand, like a cat seeking to be petted.

'For novices to our society, yes. You have to prove yourself. But you will move up through the hierarchy more quickly than most. We'll meet again, one day. And on equal terms. Then . . . who knows?'

Bending towards her, he kissed her firmly on the mouth. She responded eagerly; even her anger at his studied remoteness could not quell her ardour for him.

'Our first kiss,' she said dryly, when he drew away. 'How touching.'

He laughed. 'Oh, I knew that you were a good choice, Marika. Now. I'm going to remove your pendant. It has to be adjusted. You'll have it back in a few days.'

Sweeping her up in his strong arms, he made her comfortable and laid her head on the pillow. She heard him walk across the room and open the door. Raising herself on her elbows, she turned towards him, but before she could say anything else, he'd gone.

Swearing under her breath, she fumbled with the blindfold. He'd secured it thoroughly and it took her a few moments to undo the knot. At last it came loose. She rubbed at her eyes and the bridge of her nose, taking a moment to adjust her vision.

The first thing she saw was the black card on the pillow. It had a telephone number printed on it in gold lettering. Her heart sank for a moment. Another card. Cold, impersonal. There was nothing of Stone to savour, just the memory of the devastating sex.

Marika rose from the bed and made for the bathroom. The mirrored wardrobe showed her a woman who looked like she'd been served by an entire rugby team. Her face was flushed, her make-up smudged and her hair was all awry. The zips hung open on the leather bodice, her breasts jutted out obscenely and the light brown floss of her pubic hair peeped out from the parted zip at her groin.

She smiled and her grey eyes glittered with purpose.

'Oh, I'll be ready for you when we meet face to face, Stone,' she said aloud to her reflection. 'And when we do, *you* are in for a big surprise.'

CHAPTER

6

The pendant arrived in the post two days later. Marika opened the special delivery packet and held the pendant in her hand. She saw the difference at once. The plain jet oval now bore a carving. Two small hearts, intertwined.

She felt a quite unexpected surge of pride. It was clear that she had been accepted into the Discipline of Pearls. What her rank was, she didn't know. Pia's pendant had borne a carving of a single heart. No doubt the significance of the entwined hearts would become clear in time.

Gulping down the cooling dregs of her breakfast coffee, she grabbed for her handbag and left the flat. Gunning the BMW into life she headed towards the office. As she sat in the rush-hour traffic that clogged the Gray's Inn Road, Marika listened to a Sinead O'Connor tape. Her taste in music was eclectic, even a little old-fashioned. She preferred singers with haunting voices to the heavy throb of club music or modern rap.

When 'Nothing Compares 2 U' began playing,

she thought of Stone and was instantly in a state of heightened body awareness. Every small movement of her clothes against her skin sent little tremors of desire along her nerve ends.

Is this me, she thought, the person who loved to be in control, who couldn't let go when making love, whose emotions matched the cool, calm decor of her flat? She hardly recognised herself.

But she loved her new awareness and gloried in her burgeoning sensuality. Shaking back her loose hair, she turned up the cassette player. A biscuit-coloured Rolls Royce passed her as she drove towards Holborn and the uniformed chauffeur glanced her way. She threw him a brilliant smile and he tipped his cap to her, grinning appreciatively.

Tower Bridge slipped by on her right and she navigated her car expertly through the stream of traffic. Speeding up as she reached the Highway, Marika felt happier than she had done for weeks. There was only one black cloud on the horizon. She didn't like deceiving James, but she couldn't see any way of telling him about Stone.

In theory she and James had an open relationship, but she couldn't imagine him accepting her recent behaviour with equanimity. The fact that he was married would make no difference. He'd always insisted that his wife had nothing to do with what he and Marika shared.

Marika was aware of the irony of the situation. Dealing with James was a problem she decided to shelve and sort out later.

Gwen brought a tray of fresh coffee into the office along with Marika's appointments book.

'To soften the blow,' Gwen explained, beaming.

'You've a hectic few days ahead.'

Marika scanned the pages. She groaned. Every day for the next week was filled to capacity. Gwen had even booked lunchtime meetings. Today her first appointment was in ten minutes' time.

Pouring a cup of steaming fresh coffee, Marika smiled up at Gwen.

'Let's get to it then. Is Troy Maplethorpe here yet? He's usually on time.' Troy was a promising young cricketer, hoping to cash in on his good looks and charisma.

'Ready and waiting,' Gwen said. 'I'll tell him you're on the phone. Give you a couple of minutes to finish your coffee.'

'Thanks, Gwen,' Marika grinned.

The day passed in a whirlwind of activity. Marika arranged interviews, haggled over deals, bolstered egos, and secured a new client. Over a lunch of salad nicoise, she discussed the needs of a sales director of a fast-food chain.

By six-thirty she was ready to go home and take a long hot bath. As she was brushing her damp hair, James phoned to say that he'd be calling by. Still in her towelling bathrobe, she padded over to her wardrobe. About to pull out a pair of cream trousers and grey sweater, she paused. At the top of the wardrobe was the black cardboared box which contained the leather bodysuit.

She lifted it down from the shelf and placed it on the bed. Parting the folds of tissue paper she took the garment out. Just looking at the shiny black leather made her feel aroused. Untying the belt of the bathrobe, she let it fall to the ground.

She held the body close to her skin, looking at herself in the mirror. A faint odour of sex seemed to come from the leather. She couldn't wait to put it on.

The leather clung to her like a second skin, nipping in her waist, confining her breasts, and defining the swell of her buttocks. She loved the feel of it, the look of it on her. And the memory of the hotel room added a piquancy to her enjoyment.

She scrunch-dried her hair so that it fell around her shoulders in a soft tangle of waves. Apart from face-powder, she didn't bother with make-up. Then, on impulse, she filled in her lips with a deep red pencil and pressed them together. A pair of black Lycra hold-up stockings and high-heeled black shoes improved her appearance even more.

The mirror showed her sexy alter ego. She felt hot and erotically charged, hardly able to keep her hands from straying to her black clad groin. She itched to stroke herself, to massage her moist folds and throbbing inner membranes, but she decided to wait for James to arrive.

He'd get one big surprise. She couldn't wait to see the look on his face – surprise first, she imagined, followed swiftly by lust.

Like most men his age, James loved to see her in provocative underwear, particularly stockings and suspenders. He'd bought her gifts of silk French knickers, expensive French bras, and a rather daring black lace basque. But he'd never seen her wearing anything like this.

She looked forward to a night of pleasure. It was just what she needed to unwind. And, if she was completely honest, to ease the fire which Stone had awoken within her and which smouldered below the surface most of the time now.

It was as if she was becoming two separate

people: the high-powered professional at work and the private, sexy strong-minded woman who was prepared to take risks to slake her mounting passions. She decided that she liked her two halves; they seemed to add up to a more happy and whole self.

It had been the sensual hidden side of her personality which had suffered over the past two years. Career had come first, but that was no longer fulfilling. She had gazed into the heart of the fire, walked in the flames, and emerged purified and tempered.

Now she wanted it all. And she knew that she was strong enough to reach out and take what Stone offered.

As she grew in confidence and began to feel better about her newfound sensuality, she felt the need to 'come out' to James. She wouldn't tell him about Stone yet, if ever, but she wanted him to see that she was changing, blossoming as a complete woman.

The leather outfit might be too startling when seen in the glow of the lights, so she decided to prolong the game a little. Shrugging the towelling bathrobe back on over the leather bodysuit, she went into the kitchen and put a bottle of Chablis into the fridge. Then she went into the sitting-room and turned down the lights. She lit the candles in their Italian cast-iron holders. Selecting some slow, dreamy music she settled back to wait for James.

James embraced her and kissed her cheek.

'Mmmm. You smell nice,' he said. 'But I thought you'd be dressed. You'd just stepped out of the bath when I phoned. I've booked a table for nine, remember?'

Marika had completely forgotten that they were supposed to be dining out. Never mind, James would enjoy the dish she would present to him. She smiled wickedly and led him into the sitting-room.

'I thought we might stay in tonight,' she said. 'You can phone the restaurant and cancel, can't you?'

James glanced around the room. A slow smile came over his face.

'Looks like you've got other plans for us. Who am I to argue?'

He went into the hall and picked up the phone. Marika heard him speaking to the manager of the restaurant. She put the wine and glasses on a tray and brought it into the sitting-room. When James came back in, she handed him a glass of Chablis. He relaxed against the back of the sofa and took a sip.

'So. How was your day?' Marika said softly.

James grinned, his blue eyes crinkling. He reached out and stroked her cheek.

'Somehow I don't think you're all that interested,' he said. His voice deepened into a John Wayne drawl. 'You want my body, woman. I can tell.'

'Oh really! You do catch on quickly,' Marika laughed.

James chuckled and reached for her, but she evaded him.

'Wait a minute. I want to show you something.'

James stretched out on the sofa, his handsome face alight with interest and desire. She felt a surge of affection for him. I'll make this good for him as well as me, she thought. He won't forget tonight in a hurry.

Getting up she crossed the room. After turning the music up she came back towards the sofa. Smiling at James, she swayed gently from side to side, her lips curving in a smile that was rich with promise.

James lifted his wine glass in a toast, his eyes glistening appreciatively as he took in her stockinged calves and high-heeled shoes.

'What's this? My own private show?' he asked.

'If you like.'

Marika brought her hands slowly up the front of her body and then down again to the belt of her bathrobe. She pulled on the belt until it came undone, then held the two sides of the robe closed while she rotated her hips in a slow sensual movement.

James sat forward, his wine forgotten as she began to open the front of the bathrobe. She let the robe hang open, giving James a brief tantalising glimpse of her shiny black torso, then swung around and presented him with her back view.

Raising her hands, she lifted her hair, letting the soft, fluffy mass of it strand through her fingers. Glancing over her shoulder, she pouted at James.

She was enjoying herself so much she didn't notice that he was sitting very still, a look of mounting confusion on his face.

Marika spun around to face James, her mouth curving in a brilliant smile. Letting the robe slip down over her shoulders, she dropped it to the carpet and stood with her feet apart, her hands on her hips.

James put his wine glass on the floor. She noticed that his hand was shaking slightly. He looked her up and down slowly, his expression unreadable. He's shocked, Marika thought, but I was too when I first saw the bodysuit.

She smiled encouragingly, moved towards him, and knelt down close to the sofa. Settling herself next to his outstretched legs, she leaned against him, giving him a clear view of her shadowed cleavage and constricted waist.

James looked bemused and a little worried, but she ignored that.

'Marika . . .'

'Sh,' she whispered. 'Don't say anything yet. I want to please you. Just sit back and enjoy it.'

Reaching out her hand she slid it up his leg, feeling the texture of his grey cord trousers against her palm. Under the fabric she felt his muscled thighs. She imagined his cock, thick and sturdy, pressing against the imprisonment of his underwear.

Leaning close she brushed his cheek with her lips, breathing in the familiar smell of him – clean maleness and his favourite woody cologne. His skin was smooth and cool against her mouth.

James made a sound in his throat and moved his head back. Marika's lips slid down his cheek and grazed his chin. She chuckled softly.

'Playing hard to get, are you?'

Her hand was resting on his groin and she massaged him gently, feeling for the expected tumescence. He was soft under her hand. She was surprised. James was usually ready to go, needing no more urging that a suggestive look. Maybe he was tired and needed more direct stimulation.

The zip opened under her fingers and she slipped her hand inside James's trousers. The front slit of his boxer shorts parted and she closed her hands over his cock. James fidgeted as she began stroking him and then drew his flaccid member through the gaping fly.

Arching over him, she bent down and began to suck the soft tip, flicking the underside delicately with her tongue. There was no response. James's cock remained soft and small. If anything, she thought, it seemed to shrink.

James squirmed and she thought that he was enjoying her ministrations and beginning to relax into the pleasure of the situation. Then he placed his hands on her head and pushed her away. His touch wasn't gentle. When he let go, she could still feel the place where his fingers had pressed into her scalp.

For a moment longer, she mistook his attitude for passion. Laying her cheek against one cord-covered thigh, she reached out and encircled his waist with her arms.

'Stop that,' James said in a strangled voice. 'Get off! Just get off me, will you!'

She looked up at him in confusion, realising finally that he was furious.

'But why? What's wrong?'

'You ask me that! What the hell do you think you're doing, behaving like a tart? And what do you think you look like? Eh? All got up like . . . like some bloody high-class call girl . . . Where did you get that ridiculous outfit?'

Words seemed to fail him. He moved away from her and slid across the sofa, stuffing his cock back into his trousers as he did so. His face was set into lines of anger.

'I never imagined that we needed these sort of cheap thrills. Obviously you think there's something lacking in our relationship. Well okay, let's talk about it. But cover yourself up first, for God's sake. You look ridiculous.'

Marika remained kneeling. She looked up at James, the shock of his words settling like cold stone in her stomach. How could she have been so stupid, so wrong? She'd imagined that he was going to enjoy the experience of having her take the initiative. He'd entered into the spirit of things that time when she'd faked having a cold, despite his initial wariness.

Since then, they'd settled into their usual pattern; straight sex, which James instigated. It was unimaginative and for her unsatisfying. But that was obviously the way James wanted things to stay.

She felt the anger beginning to surface. All right, she'd made a mistake. James wasn't the free thinker he imagined himself to be, but that didn't give him licence to insult her. She looked great in the leather bodysuit and she felt even better.

She knew then, with sudden clarity, that she'd outgrown James. It wasn't just the sex. It was everything. There had always been restrictions in their relationship; his wife was the silent partner between them. She hadn't minded that. It meant that James wouldn't be tempted to get more serious. But they'd worn their relationship out. There was nowhere else for them to go.

Marika was poised on the brink of a journey of self-discovery. She knew that she had to embark on it alone.

Slowly, she pushed herself to her feet. Without speaking or glancing at James, she walked across to the coffee table and picked up her glass of wine. Taking a sip, she seated herself in the chair opposite him. With insolent slowness, she crossed one leg over the other and gave him a long measuring glance over the rim of her wine glass.

'Aren't you going to get changed?' James said, his voice sounding tight and unfamiliar. 'Christ. What *do* you look like.'

'I look great, actually,' she said coolly. 'I look like a woman who's aware of her sexuality and isn't afraid to admit to it.'

James just stared at her. Then, as he absorbed the shuttered look on her face, he changed tack.

'Look, I'm sorry if I over-reacted. I can see that you're upset. It was just a bit of fun, right? I didn't mean . . . Oh, hell. Just get dressed, love. We'll go for a walk. Salvage something of the evening.'

Marika took a sip of wine, savouring the flavour of fruit on her palate.

'I don't think so,' she said slowly. 'I think you should just leave. It's best if you don't come here again. It's over between us, James.'

James gaped at her, the colour draining from his cheeks.

'You can't be serious. That's it? Right out of the blue, with no warning? Just because I don't like you wearing that . . . that . . . leather thing?'

'No. Not because of that. I just think it's time. We're going nowhere, James. I think we should face that.'

He didn't believe that she was serious at first, but after an hour of discussion he realised that she meant what she said. He promised to phone her in a few days to see whether she'd changed her mind.

'You do that,' she said to him at the door, knowing that she was making the right decision.

She felt sad when he had gone. It would take some time to adjust to not having him around. She knew now that she ought to have finished with James long ago, but he was part of the life she had planned so meticulously for herself.

Now she was free of all encumbrances. Free to explore the new possiiblities, those which membership of the secret society had opened up for her.

She went into her bedroom and glanced at herself in the wardrobe mirror. Running her fingertips over her leather-clad curves, she imagined that she could feel the leashed tension within her pushing at her spread digits. The hot throbbing of her vulva was echoed in the heavy, swollen feeling in her breasts.

Opening a drawer she took out a vibrator and went to kneel beside her bed. Leaning forward, she unzipped the leather crotch of the bodysuit and spread her thighs in the way that Stone had done. Imagining Stone's hands on her, his cock in her, she pleasured herself with the vibrator.

With the blunt plastic head, she nudged her folds apart and pressed gently on her throbbing clit. Smoothing the rounded head over the little nub of flesh, she coaxed it from its tiny hood. Her clit seemed to swell and ache under the direct pressure and she moved the head of the vibrator backwards to the entrance of her vagina.

She teased herself by inserting the vibrator just a little way inside at first, loving the way her sex-flesh seemed to suck and pull at the plastic as she moved it back and forth. Then she couldn't wait any longer. She needed to feel penetrated.

'Oh yes,' she moaned, as she pushed the plastic shaft deeply inside herself.

While the ticklish vibrations spread outwards from the moist walls of her vagina, she pinched and rolled one nipple, squeezing hard until slivers of pain added their spice to the pleasure that filled her.

She moaned and writhed as she came, thrusting the buzzing vibrator deeply into her warm, wet inner-darkness. She came twice before she was satisfied, marvelling at her ability to orgasm so easily.

Afterwards she lay on the bed, gazing up at the ceiling, idly stroking herself. The truth had finally dawned on her. Membership of the Discipline of Pearls was no longer a luxury, an option to be explored at her leisure. It had become so much more.

In fact, it was a necessity. A lifeline, something she couldn't imagine not having.

A slow, contented smile curved her mouth. How did you know, Stone? she thought. One day I'll ask you that.

The gold letters on the card stood out starkly against the black background.

Marika held the phone, listening to the dialling tone, her pulses racing as she waited for the sound of the disembodied voice at the other end of the line.

'Good evening. Marika, is it not?'

This time it was a woman, her voice mature and cultured. She had an accent which Marika could not quite place. European, she decided. Marika had hoped it would be Stone. She stifled her disappointment.

'Yes. It's Marika. How did you know it was me?' she asked.

'I do not normally permit questions, but you have earned the right to some answers,' the woman said. 'Those who wear the intertwined heart are destined for great things.'

She paused, allowing Marika to absorb her words. So the carving on her pendant marked her out as someone special? Marika felt a small thrill at the thought of it.

'You are the only person to have been given this particular number,' the woman went on. 'In that way, we keep track of who is meeting whom. That is all I can tell you at present. Now, here are your instructions.'

Marika was to go to Paris. A package, containing tickets and instructions, would arrive in the post.

'This is satisfactory?' the woman asked.

'Perfectly. Thank you.' Marika rang off.

She felt the urge to speak to Pia, to ask for more information about the Discipline of Pearls. Perhaps Pia had heard something about Stone by now. If not, then she certainly must know why Marika's pendant bore a double heart.

On impulse, she dialled the model's home number. There was no reply, just an answerphone. Marika left a message for Pia to call her when she got back.

She found that she missed James more than she expected to and had to resist the urge to contact him. She knew that it was best that they parted and a clean break was kinder in the long run. She informed Gwen of the situation and asked her to say that she was in a business meeting if James called.

James did phone the office a few times and she finally agreed to talk to him. Their conversation was short and predictable. Marika insisting that they were finished, James not believing it.

'If I repeat myself often enough, he'll get the message in the end,' she said to Gwen.

'Poor man,' Gwen said. 'You sure about this?'

'Absolutely certain,' Marika said.

Gwen eyed her warily. 'You're different lately. There's something about you. Have you got someone else?'

Marika coloured and changed the subject. Gwen knew her far too well.

The package arrived the next day. Inside Marika found a return ticket to Paris and a short letter.

'A car will meet you at Charles de Gaulle Airport and take you to an address. When your assignation is complete you will be transported back to the airport.'

She was to fly out late Friday night, in two day's time. Not for the first time she wondered who was financing her trips. There must be some powerful people involved in the organisation.

Marika went to work at the office in a fever of excitement. It was difficult for her to concentrate, but by a sheer effort of will she managed to apply herself to the work in hand.

At two p.m. on Friday afternoon, she met Janice Clements at Broadcasting House and sat with her in a small soundproofed room, while Janice was interviewed about her book via telephone link-ups.

Somehow Marika concentrated on what Janice was saying, although her mind was full of the Paris trip and what that might bring. It was four-thirty before Janice finished her interviews.

Complimenting her on her professionalism,

Marika escorted Janice out of the building and hailed a cab for her.

By the time she arrived back at the office and dealt with a mountain of paperwork, battled with rush-hour traffic and reached her flat it was almost seven p.m. Too excited to eat, she bathed, washed her hair, and dressed in a black, figured velvet skirt-suit.

Running her hands down her hips, she smoothed the short skirt down over a black satin slip. The straight skirt skimmed her knees. It was perfectly plain at the front, but at the centre back there was a deep kick-pleat. The fitted jacket buttoned high to the neck and had unlined sleeves of heavy black lace.

High-heeled black ankle boots completed her outfit.

The letter had not made it clear how long she would be staying in Paris. Assuming that it could be overnight or for a couple of days at most, she packed a small case with toiletries, clean underwear and a change of clothes. She took a cab to Heathrow and arrived in plenty of time to check in for her flight.

It was eleven-thirty by the time she was seated and looking out of the plane window at the lights of London. As the plane climbed into the clear sky, she closed her eyes and tried to calm her nerves.

The flight was smooth and trouble-free. As she walked out of the main entrance of Charles de Gaulle, she saw the uniformed chauffeur holding up the card with her name on it.

The chauffeur's eyes swept over her slim form, taking in her upswept fair hair and the gold and onyx drop earrings. She smiled tightly as he held the car door open for her.

Settling back against the leather seat of the limousine, Marika relaxed as the big car cruised towards the Rue de la Chapelle Dormoy and headed south into the heart of Paris. The car smelt of leather polish and Gitanes.

There was a hot core of excitement in her stomach. She had no idea what to expect, but that fact added a piquancy to her fear. She looked out through the tinted windows at the night-time streets. They drove for about an hour.

She knew parts of Paris, but her visits had been limited to the fashionable areas. She did not recognise the narrow streets they were cruising along now.

Pools of light from street-lamps illuminated cobbled lanes. Here and there she glimpsed iron railings and steep steps leading up to shadowed alleyways. Thickly blossomed trees looked ghostly in the moonlight. The car slipped smoothly down the silent streets, turning onto open squares where the dark shapes of roosting pigeons decorated the tall, narrow-fronted houses, like living carvings.

The limousine stopped at the entrance to one of the many featureless alleyways. Marika stepped out onto the wet pavement, the clean scent of rain filling her nostrils. She looked around. The brick walls that lined the narrow alleyway seemed to be smooth and featureless. There were no houses on either side, just shuttered shops.

'Where am I to go?' she asked the chauffeur.

He shrugged.

'I was told to leave you here, *mademoiselle,*' he said in French. 'I will return for you in two hours.'

With that, he stepped into the car and drove away. Marika started forward. Perhaps there was a doorway set in the alley wall, invisible from the street. The single lamp at the far end of the alley gave out a faint light.

Heart beating fast she walked into the shadow-printed darkness, the heels of her ankle boots ringing on the cobbles. About halfway down the alley, she saw that there was a door – or rather a sort of sliding metal sheet.

Set in the wall to one side of the metal 'door' was a panel with a push-button bell and a small grille. Marika pressed the button and spoke into the grille. The metal sheet slid open and she stepped inside.

Immediately she was asasulted by a wall of noise, the harsh throbbing beat of some kind of industrial music. A haze of smoke floated on the air. Figures twisted and gyrated on a spotlit dance floor, most of them wearing very little. A tall red-haired woman wore a halter made of chains which exposed her nipples. Another was bare-breasted. A man, who she thought wore trousers, turned around and she saw that his buttocks were bare.

Ill at ease, Marika glanced towards the far end of the room, which was in shadow. She was able to make out a bar. After the flight and the car journey, she felt in need of a drink. Making her way towards the bar, she saw that there were side rooms leading off from the dance area. In one of them people sat at tables, talking and laughing.

It was not what she had expected and she felt a sense of disappointment. This was obviously some sort of exclusive club. Was she supposed to mingle with these strangers? People she probably had nothing in common with? She had been hoping to see Stone – face to face this time – but she realised that it was most unlikely.

Somewhat dispirited she ordered a Pernod and blackcurrant, then sat on a bar stool watching the dancers as she drank it. She turned at the touch of a hand on her arm.

'Pia!' she said at once, delighted to see the beautiful model again. 'What are you doing here? I phoned you a few days ago and left a message. Did you get it?'

Pia smiled and shook her head.

'I haven't been in London lately. I had an assignment in Paris. The Prêt-à-Porter Spring collections, but I've finished for now. I'm here tonight for the same reason you are.'

'You know why I'm here?'

Pia nodded, her dark eyes glittering with excitement. 'Oh yes. Come with me.'

Marika picked up her drink and followed Pia. She felt happier, having met up with her friend. Pia was the only person she could talk to about the secret society. Pia led her through a door that led to a sort of dressing-room.

The room was small, the walls stained and yellowish. There was a mirror, a tattered screen, two chairs, and a wash basin. On a dress rail hung various outfits made of leather and other fabrics, mainly coloured red or black.

Pia sank onto one of the chairs and indicated that Marika should sit on the other. Marika studied the model. Her sleek dark hair had been teased into a spiky halo. She wore a dusky lipstick, which looked striking against her olive skin. Her dark eyes were smudged with smoky grey shadow and black liner emphasised their natural tilt.

Pia's dress was a mere wisp of silver satin with

shoestring traps. Her high round breasts, narrow waist and long slim legs were all shown to advantage.

Marika experienced another of those little jolts of envy. She felt guilty, because she liked Pia. It was just that Pia was so damned perfect-looking.

'You look good,' Pia said. 'Black suits you.'

'Thanks,' Marika said, feeling even more guilty for her uncharitable thoughts. She glanced around the horrible little room, wrinkling her nose with disdain.

'What is this place?'

'This is where we're to get ready,' Pia said.

Marika gaped at her. 'Ready for what?'

'You really don't know? Didn't you get any instructions with your air ticket?'

'Just that I would be brought to a destination by car.'

Pia smiled slowly, her full red lips parting to show perfect teeth.

'We're to put on a floor show this evening. You and I are the main attraction.'

CHAPTER

7

Marika stared blankly at Pia, not quite understanding what she meant.

'Floor show? But I can't sing or dance. What are we supposed to do?'

Pia smiled slowly. When she answered her voice was low-pitched and tense with excitement.

'Anything we like. And it isn't dancing they have in mind. At least, not unless it's a very erotic routine. These people are sophisticated. Connoisseurs of sensuality. Let's shock them, shall we?'

She stood up and moved across to Marika. Her slim thigh pressed against Marika's lace-clad arm. Leaning down she pressed her full lips to Marika's cheek.

Marika jumped as if she'd been burned and Pia laughed, the sound soft and husky.

'For someone who's earned herself the entwined heart, you're very innocent. Almost virginal, in fact.'

Marika coloured. Pia was younger than her by eight years or so, but in this situation Pia exuded an air of mature sophistication. Pia was right, Marika did feel out of her depth, but she was determined to give a good account of herself. If Pia felt up to taking on this latest challenge, then she did too.

Marika took a deep breath to steady her nerves. This was the most nerve-wracking thing she'd had to do so far; far worse than allowing the masked man to spank her and worse than going to the hotel and meeting Stone.

She watched Pia as she began sorting through the clothes which hung on the rail. Pia glanced at Marika.

'Since you seem to have decided to see this through, it might be a good idea to get changed. We'll probably get some ideas while we do that.'

She pulled out a hanger which held what looked like a tangled mass of straps and buckles. Throwing the outfit onto the chair, she took hold of the hem of her dress and lifted it over her head in one swift movement.

Marika coloured and tried not to stare. Apart from silver-sheened tights and the tiniest white lace tanga, Pia was naked. Her breasts were small and round, the nipples neat and dark in colour. Though very slim, with a tiny waist, she was curvy. Her hips sloped down to taut round buttocks, bisected by a single white thong.

Pia took off her strappy shoes and tights, then stepped out of the tanga. Her pubic hair had been shaved at the sides and only a line of dark floss remained to mask the division of her sex. Hands on hips, she faced Marika as if challenging her to examine her body.

Pia's dark eyes narrowed as she smiled. She looked amused, self-assured, and confident.

Marika swallowed, her mouth dry. She knows

that she's beautiful, she thought, and she knows that I'm affected by her nudity. In fact Marika was confused by her own reactions. She'd never found a woman attractive in *that* way before.

Pia lifted the outfit, which seemed more like a harness, and held it out to Marika.

'I think you'll have to help me get into this,' she said. 'Do you mind?'

Marika rose from the chair, her mind in a turmoil. What the hell *were* they expected to do out there? But in her heart she already knew. Oh God, I don't know if I can do this, she thought with one part of her mind, but the other, newly awakened part of her was urging her on, anticipating the heady and sensory delights to come.

Her fingers trembled slightly as she began to buckle the confection of straps and buckles around Pia's slim body.

This outfit was more daring by far than the leather bodysuit Marika had worn in the hotel. It revealed more flesh than it covered, providing tantalising glimpses of pale limbs and rounded breasts and buttocks.

Marika saw that most of the things hanging on the rail looked as skimpy as the harness Pia had chosen. She dreaded having to wear something so revealing and having so many eyes studying her.

Pia's body was perfect, a living clothes-horse, but Marika was curvier, a lot heavier at breast and hip. She might appear ridiculous. Trying not to think about that, she lifted Pia's chosen outfit over her head.

The arrangement of black leather straps fitted over Pia's shoulders and encased her ribs. Her breasts were lifted and thrust into prominence by the thick strap which buckled under them. Two thinner straps, attached at the waist, passed between Pia's legs and buckled at the small of her back.

Each of these straps was shaped, so that it passed to the side of her sex, pressing and separating each of her lightly furred lips and exposing the moist, rosy folds within. As Pia moved her legs apart and adjusted the fitting of the straps between her legs, Marika couldn't help catching the faint intimate scene of her; clean, musky and tantalising.

To cover her confusion, Marika stood up and moved around to Pia's back and began fiddling with the straps to adjust the fit. When Pia was ready, she turned around, admiring herself in the fly-spotted mirror. Raising her hands, she mussed her hair so that it stood up around her head in even more pronounced spikes.

Turning to Marika, she grinned.

'Your turn now. Shall I choose for you? I have a good eye. It's my profession, after all.'

Marika nodded. Her mouth was dry. Had Stone had a hand in planning this venture? Perhaps he wanted to push her to the limit, to see what she was capable of.

That thought gave her strength. She wouldn't be beaten by him. When Pia brought the chosen outfit over to her, Marika hardly gave it a glance. It seemed to be something made of black shiny fabric and it looked very small.

Lifting her hands, she began unfastening her suit jacket. The skirt fell in a heap to the floor and she kicked off her ankle boots. Soon she wore only her black lacy bra and French knickers, her suspender belt and sheer black stockings.

'Just take your bra off,' Pia said. 'The knickers and stockings will look good worn with this.'

She held up a boned corset, made of black satin ribbons. As Pia fitted it around her ribcage. Marika realised that the corset was shaped to leave her breasts free. When the front busk was fastened, Pia began lacing up the back, pulling and adjusting the laces until Marika's waist was drawn in so tightly that she was forced to hold herself very straight and to take shallow breaths.

'Look at yourself,' Pia said. 'You look wonderful.'

Marika moved over to the mirror. She almost gasped. Her waist looked almost as tiny as Pia's and her uncovered breasts jutted out pertly, supported and enhanced by the pressure of the corset's shaped top. The black lace French knickers formed a sort of frill under the bottom of the corset and her long legs looked elegant in the sheer black Lycra.

Pia sorted through a box which lay under the dress rail and brought out a pair of strappy sandals.

'These look like your size,' she said, kneeling down to slip them onto Marika's feet.

They were a half size too big, but Marika was pleased with the effect. Her legs looked slim and shapely, the four inch heels on the black patent sandals forcing her calves to tighten and tipping her slightly forward onto the balls of her feet.

'Perfect,' Pia said when she had pinned Marika's blonde hair into a pleat. 'Except for one thing. Pinch your nipples, Marika. They are so striking – lovely and dark, unusual in someone as fair as you are. It would be good to make them erect.'

Marika brought her hands up slowly, her face flaming. She knew it was ridiculous to feel shy – soon enough there would be many eyes on her – but somehow it was impossible to stroke herself in front of Pia.

Pia laughed huskily.

'Your modesty is so sweet. Allow me,' she said and her long slender fingers closed around Marika's breasts, stroking the full, uplifted globes.

'When you perform on the catwalk, you get used to nudity and using all sorts of tricks to make yourself look good. Hold still now while I give you a tweak or two. This is just like work to me.'

But not to me, Marika thought, having to control the sharp intake of her breath as Pia stroked and pinched her nipples until the firm, red-brown cones jutted out proudly. Glancing down, Marika saw that they looked as hard and shiny as beads.

Outside in the seething darkness of the club, the music changed tone, the beat becoming strident and sensual.

'That's our cue,' Pia said, taking hold of Marika's hand and pulling her towards the door.

Marika felt sick. Cold chills seemed to trickle down her back. She pulled against Pia's hand, but Pia tightened her grip.

'I can't do this,' Marika whispered. 'I really can't. I'm going to throw up.'

'No you're not,' Pia said firmly. 'Take a few deep breaths. Okay now? Come on then. We go down this corridor to the side of the stage. You'll be fine – you'll enjoy it once we start. Now, just leave everything to me and follow my lead.'

* * *

The stage was dark and Marika almost stumbled in the high-heeled sandals.

Pia stepped out confidently, coming to a halt beside a leather-covered chaise longue. Whispering instructions to Marika, she moved back into the shadows. Marika lay back, resting her head against the studded, rolled arm of the couch, just as Pia had told her.

She closed her eyes, waiting with bated breath for the lights to go up. She became aware of a slight chemical smell and opened her eyes to see that plumes of smoke were rolling across the stage. At the same time, a wash of pink-tinged light came from above her head.

The music faded to just a background rumble of base notes. It was a slow and sensual beat, insistent and haunting. Marika felt the echo of it in her quickening pulses. She could smell cigarette smoke and a mixture of perfumes – body heat, hot leather and the sharper scent of her own nervous sweat.

Beyond the dimly lit stage, the rest of the club was in darkness, except for the glow of tiny lamps on tables. She glimpsed pale faces and shadowy figures, all of them intent on watching the stage – watching her. Trying to ignore the fact that the club was crowded, she yawned and stretched as if she had just woken up.

Pia's hurried instructions were imprinted on her mind,

'Just pretend to wake up. Imagine that you're alone and still groggy. Stretch and squirm about a bit. I'll pretend to be surprised to find you there. We'll take it from there. Don't worry. You'll love it,' Pia had said.

Marika had no choice but to fall in with Pia's plan. She had no ideas of her own. Having something to do loosened the awful numbing fear which seemed composed of too many elements for close examination. If she thought too much, she knew that she'd get up and run.

Arching her back, Marika ran her hands down the front of her body, feeling the smooth satin of the corset and the shaped boning which held her ribs and waist captive. There was a ripple of applause as she turned to the front and the audience gazed at her bare breasts.

Marika felt a surge of confidence. They liked her. She heard someone close to the stage whisper one word.

'Beautiful.'

Another voice, masculine and low-pitched, said, 'What gorgeous nipples.'

Feeling bolder and slightly less frightened, she lifted her arms and stretched again, the action lifting her breasts into even greater prominence. Her nipples were erect and hard, partly from Pia's ministrations and partly from the new excitement which was gathering in her lower belly. For the first time in her life she was glad that her nipples were so big and dark.

She caught a movement from the corner of her eye and knew that Pia had stepped out of the shadows at the back of the stage. Marika pretended that she hadn't seen her and lay back against the padded arm, one arm draped over the back of the chaise longue and her eyes half-closed as if dozing.

The applause came again as Pia walked up to the couch and stood looking down at the 'sleeping' Marika.

Marika could see through her parted lashes that Pia was pretending to be delighted and astonished. She reached out her hand and stroked Marika's hair. Bending down, she drew the pins free and allowed the blonde tresses to fan out across the leather upholstery.

Pia's fingers threaded through the pale strands of Marika's hair. Marika moved slightly as Pia's warm fingers massaged her scalp and stroked the white column of her neck.

'Lie still,' Pia whispered. 'Pretend that you're still asleep.'

She began stroking Marika's bare shoulders and the bulging flesh of her cleavage, glancing over her shoulder for the audience's approval. Her expression was that of a naughty child who cannot resist temptation. Appreciative laughter rippled towards the stage as Marika moaned and adjusted her position.

'That's it. Good,' Pia whispered. 'Lie on your back, with both hands behind your head. Now, bend one leg and rest your foot on the floor.'

Marika did so, her knee bent up by the height of the heel that rested on the wooden boards of the stage. Pia's touch was feather-light and pleasant as it travelled down her bare arms and back up to shoulders. Giving the audience another of her covert, bold glances, Pia closed both hands around Marika's breasts and massaged them in a circular motion.

There were murmurs of approval from the crowd. Marika's intake of breath was not faked this time. Pia's palms were chafing her erect nipples and little flares of sensation were spreading downwards to her groin.

She made a murmur of protest, but the sound

was cut off abruptly by the pressure of Pia's lips against her own.

Pia's hands continued to move in that maddening, rolling rhythm as her soft mouth pressed more urgently against Marika's lips. A cloud of sweet musky perfume enfolded her.

Marika was too shocked to pull away at first and by the time she realised that she was enjoying the kiss, it was too late to protest. Pia's tongue slipped between her parted lips and Marika sucked at it as it thrust assertively into her mouth.

If she closed her eyes, it was just like kissing a man, except that Pia was kissing her more soundly than any man ever had. A little moan rose in Marika's throat as Pia took her nipples between finger and thumb and pinched and rolled them, hard. Splinters of pleasure and pain spread right through her, causing her to arch against Pia and part her thighs wantonly.

It was another shock, to feel Pia's slim fingers on the inside of her thigh, but this time it was a welcome one. Marika allowed her thighs to fall open, as Pia trailed her fingers up the exposed skin above her stocking top. In another moment she jerked involuntarily as she felt the hand slip inside the loose leg of her French knickers.

Pia continued to kiss her, her tongue plunging into the hot cavern of her mouth with insistent firmness. Marika kissed her back, any reticence lost as she tasted Pia and enjoyed the texture of her lips and mouth.

The pleasure of the kiss seemed to be echoed in the tense, puffy flesh of her sex. It was pulsing in time to the stabs against the soft flesh of her mouth. Marika squirmed against the leather of the couch. Warm and pliant from her body heat it sucked at her skin, adding its own note of sensation to the tension which was building, building.

Oh God, she'd never imagined that it could feel so good to make love with a woman. As the sensuality of the thing took hold of her, demanded absolute concentration of all her senses, she became distanced from the stage, the club, the faces which were studying them both so intently.

Only Pia mattered. Beautiful, sexy and strongly aroused Pia. She realised now that this moment had been inevitable. There had been that unique spark between them from the first moment they met.

When she felt Pia's fingers stroking the silky curls on her pubis, Marika surged against her hand. Her eyes were still tightly closed and her arms raised above her head, her wrists trailing over the studded arm of the couch. As Pia applied a little more pressure to her sex, rubbing her in a circular motion, Marika shuddered and clenched both fists.

Pia smiled against her mouth as if enjoying the power she had to arouse her. Marika swooped her head around to capture Pia's mouth, grinding down onto her, grunting with passion and the anticipation of a more intimate touch on her aching sex.

She wanted something more than gentleness. She wanted to be filled, pushed into, opened and penetrated. And thrusting fingers would do nicely for now.

Pia drew away from a moment and a collective sigh rose from the audience. She knelt on the wooden stage floor and slid her hands up the outside of Marika's thighs. Taking hold of the French knickers she drew them down to Marika's calves. Encircling her slim ankles, she lifted each fetish-clad foot in turn so that she could pull the scrap of lacy silk free.

'Sit up now, my sweet,' she whispered to Marika. 'Rest back against the couch and open your legs wide.'

She smiled at Marika's look of horror and kissed the corner of her mouth.

'You want me to pleasure you, don't you. Well all these people want to see you come. They want to see you gasp and writhe and to watch as your juices flow over my fingers. Mmmm. Doesn't that sound wonderful?'

Horrified and excited by the prospect and by Pia's quietly insistent voice, Marika moved until she was sitting up, her head lolling back and her arms resting along the padded back of the couch.

Pia sat beside her. Bending her head, she took one of Marika's nipples into her mouth and sucked on it gently. Marika bucked against the warm leather that clung to her bare buttocks, feeling the supple hide release her flesh with reluctance.

With one hand Pia spread Marika's thighs wide, then wider, urging her to splay her legs.

'Come on, my love. Open as wide as you can,' she whispered.

Marika did so reluctantly, knowing that everyone in the audience could see the moist and engorged folds of her sex. The cheeks of her bottom parted too and the warm leather pressed against her anus.

Then Pia's fingers spread her labia open and

smoothed the silky moisture over her throbbing clitoral hood. Marika felt the tender lips pressed back, so that her clitoris was forced to stand proud of the surrounding folds. Her vagina pulsed, gaping open receptively.

Marika had never felt so laid bare, so exposed.

She almost sobbed with shame as she writhed and pushed herself towards Pia's hand. Her legs lolled loosely apart, the heels of her sandals digging into the floor, slanting towards each other.

The hot, smoky air of the club seemed to caress her skin and waft across her spread sex. Oh, it was hateful to be put on show in this way, to know that countless eyes were glued to her oozing, pulsing orifice. But it was so arousing to be the centre of attention, to have Pia stroking and sucking and kissing her to ultimate pleasure.

Pia's fingers, slippery now, slid up and down in a scissor movement either side of her clit. The subtle movement tipped Marika over and she climaxed, her hips thrusting lewdly into the air, pumping and working beyond her control.

'Oh God,' she gasped. 'Oh yes. Yes . . . Pia. Oh God.'

She heard the sighs and murmurs from the audience and knew that some of them, aroused by her visible pleasure, had arranged themselves into similar erotic couplings.

Marika thought that her pleasure had peaked, but she was wrong. Pia slid to the floor in front of her and began lapping at her soaking folds with her tongue. Beside herself Marika moaned and grunted, not caring now who watched her as waves of exquisite sensation spread throughout her body.

She climaxed again and again, spreading her legs as wide as possible and pushing her engorged sex against Pia's willing mouth.

When Marika surfaced and came back to herself, she saw that the lights in the main body of the club were a little brighter. The music was once again thudding out in a vibrant, impersonal rhythm. It seemed that the show was over.

She could see that men and women were spread over the tables, their partners thrusting into willing orifices or bending between spread thighs to do them fleshly homage. A large woman with pendulous breasts was holding a young man on her lap, one hand masturbating him while he suckled her.

One man sitting alone and gazing intently at the stage caught her eye. His stillness was what made him stand out. All around, people were engaged in every sex act possible, but he ignored them all.

Marika recognised him at once. Those saturnine features and cold, measuring eyes were unmistakable.

Stone.

He had come here for her. She felt an unexpected surge of joy. Bringing her legs together, she sat up. Pia made a sound of disappointment and reached for her. Marika glanced down at the kneeling woman. She smiled and reached out a hand to stroke her perfect olive cheek.

'Don't go away. There's something I have to do. It won't take long.'

'Please hurry back. I'm so horny I think I'll die if I don't come soon.' Pia's eyes were moist with longing and Marika felt a surge of tenderness towards her.

She brushed Pia's full red lips with her own.

'Wait for me in the dressing-room. Don't get dressed.'

Pia grinned. 'I won't.'

Marika stood up and hurried to the side of the stage, where steps led down into the club. She made her way across the room, ignoring the voices which congratulated her and the hands which patted her sweat-slicked skin.

Even before she reached the table where Stone had been sitting, she saw that it was empty. All there was left of him was a glass containing the milky yellow dregs of his Pernod. Then she saw the black card which he'd slipped under the glass.

She picked it up. There was the usual gold embossed telephone number.

Once again, there was nothing of him. Just the impersonal black card. There was a taste like ashes in her mouth. Whirling around, she strode through the club and found her way to the back room.

Pia was waiting. She held out her arms to Marika and they embraced. When Pia kissed her, Marika tasted her own intimate musk. Pia pressed her body up against Marika and ground her hips into her. Pushing one leg between Marika's thighs, she rubbed against Marika's naked crotch.

When Marika didn't respond, she pulled away.

'What is it? What's wrong?'

'I . . . don't know. I'm sorry, Pia. Can we get out of here?' I've had enough of this place. Is there somewhere we can go to relax? Maybe take a bath?'

'Of course. No problem. We can go to my hotel.' Her red mouth curved in a smile. 'I've a suite of rooms. And a king-size bed with satin sheets, all to myself. There's champagne and pâté de foie gras in the fridge.'

'Sounds wonderful,' Marika said with feeling. 'Come on, I'll help you dress.'

The limousine was waiting outside the club. Pia gave the chauffeur directions and the car edged away from the curb and slipped into the Paris streets.

Pia leaned back against the seat. She was dressed in a burgundy velvet evening cloak with a deep ruched collar. Her slender neck and neat head, protruding from the folds of richly coloured velvet, made her look fragile and waif-like.

'Why did you run off like that, back at the club?' she asked Marika.

Marika smiled.

'I saw Stone in the audience,' she said dryly. 'I wanted to speak to him. When I reached his table, he'd gone. I found this though.'

Pia stared at the card. She looked up at Marika, her tilted dark eyes wide with surprise.

'It was him? You're absolutely sure?'

'Yes. Certain. Why? You sound shocked.'

Pia shook her head, a bemused expression on her face.

'He's breaking all the rules. I'm supposed to give you a card and make the necessary contacts for your next assignment. There has to be an element of uncertainty. The unknown, the spice of danger, is what adds so much to our sexual pleasure. Stone's getting too involved. He shouldn't have been there tonight. He shouldn't even know what you were doing.'

Marika told her about her assignation at the London hotel.

Pia pursed her lips in a whistle.

'And you think that it was him who blindfolded

you and took you from behind?'

'I know it was him,' Marika said. 'I recognised his voice and his smell. There was no mistake.'

Pia was quiet for a moment. The car sped through the silent streets.

'I don't know what's going on,' she said finally. 'But I've got a suspicion that Stone is one of the elders – one of those who founded the Discipline of Pearls. I've never met any of them, but I've met someone occasionally who has. The elders are a law unto themselves. That has to be it. There's no way Stone could get away with acting like he is, unless he's a powerful influence within the society. And there's something else. Something I didn't tell you earlier.'

'What's that?'

Pia looked at her from the tail of her eye.

'It's about your pendant. I wasn't going to say anything, because . . . well to tell you the truth, I was jealous.'

'Jealous of me? But why?'

It seemed incredible to Marika that Pia should be jealous of anybody. She had everything going for her – looks, status, a glamorous life-style that many women would envy, and a huge salary.

Pia gave her a shaky smile. 'I've got over the jealousy now. After tonight I . . . feel close to you. And I'm glad that you're being singled out for special treatment.'

She took a deep breath. 'The intertwined heart motif puts you in a new league. It elevates you to a position of some power within the society. I'm not sure exactly what it means, but you have the right to ask questions and demand answers. No one will challenge your right to go your own way if you wish to.'

She snuggled up to Marika and laid her head on her shoulder.

'For example, you could stay on with me in Paris for a few days,' she said.

'I'll think about it,' Marika said, knowing that was exactly what she would do. Pia was too irresistible to brush off lightly.

Slipping her hand into her handbag, she took out the pendant. Pia watched her as she studied the carving of the interwined hearts.

'I've only achieved single heart status and I've been in the society for almost two years,' she said thoughtfully, with no trace of rancour, turning her face up to Marika. 'You've been marked out, Marika. There's something special about you. I felt it the first time we met.'

She laughed, as if glad that the difficult subject had been broached and then set aside.

'Who knows. Maybe you've been marked out to become an elder too. Wouldn't that be something?'

Pia rested her hand on Marika's velvet-covered thigh. Marika covered Pia's hand with her own, returning the pressure of the slim fingers.

As the car reached the centre of Paris and headed towards Montparnasse, Marika ran her fingertips over the carving. The jet was warm beneath her fingers.

If I'm really so special, she thought, why does Stone avoid confronting me?

CHAPTER 8

Marika awoke to find sunshine pouring in through the black and white floor-length curtains of Pia's hotel bedroom.

Pia had drawn them back the night before and Marika could see the slate-blue roof tops of Paris, so distinctive with their many attic windows and little red chimneys. The early morning mist was already changing from blue to champagne.

Marika lay still for a moment, savouring the view. It was that rich glow of northern light which gave Paris its magic and which had appealed to painters down the ages.

After a while she stretched and turned over, curving herself around Pia's still sleeping form. Her bent knees cupped Pia's buttocks and she slid one hand up the slender waist and closed it on one breast.

Pia stirred, turned into Marika's embrace, and kissed her passionately.

'Good morning, darling,' she murmured against Marika's lips. 'What shall we do today? Stay in bed? I could ring room service and have fresh coffee, croissants and strawberry confiture sent up.'

Marika had other plans. She kissed the tip of Pia's nose, then pulled back the black satin sheets, smiling at Pia's cry of dismay as her pale limbs were uncovered.

'Up you get, lazybones! I don't intend to waste a day in Paris,' she laughed. 'I love this city too much. I'm going to stroll down the Rue de Rivoli to that little park behind the Palais Royal and wander around the Galleries Colbert and Vivienne. Then I think I'll reward myself with lunch at the Café de la Paix.'

Pia pulled a face.

'Shopping, then lunch?'

Marika nodded. 'I only brought one change of clothes. I need to buy some things. I didn't expect to stay on for more than a few hours. I wasn't to know that I'd meet up with someone so tantalising that she'd keep me in Paris for days on end.'

Pia grinned, showing her perfect teeth.

'Flatterer! Oh, all right. I'll come with you. Next to sex, my favourite thing is buying beautiful things. Promise that we can cross the Seine by the Pont des Arts. I adore that flowery little bridge.'

'Whatever you like.'

Marika tipped up Pia's chin and kissed the soft pursed mouth. The perfection of Pia's mouth fascinated her. Without lipstick, Pia's lips were dark-pink in colour and with a clear outline. They were as full and sensual as the young Bardot's. She drew away for a moment and ran her fingertip over the pouting bottom lip.

'Besides,' she mused, 'now that I've decided that I'm not going to hurry back to London, we'll have all evening and the whole night to make love.'

Pia clasped her tightly, pressing the length of her slim body against Marika's fuller form. They kissed again. Pia's lips opened under Marika's and her tongue slipped into her mouth. Marika's breath quickened as slim hands slid down to caress her bottom. Questing fingers slid into the moist valley between her buttocks and began to toy with her pubic curls.

When Pia's caresses became more insistent, her fingertips probing into the parting of her sex, Marika pulled away. She smiled down into the tilted dark eyes which seemed drugged by passion.

'Oh no you don't. I'm not being seduced by those tactics! Out of bed, you, if you're coming with me. Right now! And into the shower.'

They showered together, spreading creamy, sweet-scented foam over each other's skin. Despite Marika's protestations, she found her pulses quickening as the heady scent of orchids filled the bathroom and Pia's slim hands described slippery circles on her skin. Pia's limbs were smooth and rounded under her palms.

Marika sagged against the art nouveau tiles, her knees gaping as Pia's fingers worked their sensual magic on her intimate folds. Arching her back, the tension rising in her, she moaned as she reached for her peak of pleasure. Pia bent over her, her small nipples grazing back and forth across Marika's stiffly erect nubs.

Pia's fingers plunged deeply into Marika's vagina, sliding in and out of her, while the pad of her thumb rubbed Marika's swollen clit. Marika cried out as she came, her teeth closing on the lobe of Pia's ear. Then the sound of her cries was caught and trapped by Pia's covering mouth as she twisted to possess Marika again.

Still kissing they edged out of the shower and into the bedroom. Not caring that the satin sheets became damp from their wet bodies, they writhed on the huge bed. Interlocked at arms and legs, they thrashed out their passion, then pleasured each other in a more leisurely way with lips and tongues.

Marika was astonished that she so savoured the sweet, musky taste of Pia's sex. Having discovered the delights to be had in loving a woman, now she wanted to explore them to the full. Pia was a feast of delights for the hand and eye. Her sex was a neat oval-shape and beautifully formed.

Marika loved kneeling between Pia's wide-spread thighs and spreading open the deep-pink folds with her fingertips. She drank in the sight of the delicately frilled flesh, edged with the lightest fringe of dark curls, and the eager, shadowed vagina. Pia's sex pulsed with passion and was moist with her juices.

Marika bent her head and teased the jutting clit with flicks of her tongue. When Pia moaned and tossed her head from side to side, Marika sucked the hard little protuberance into her mouth and frigged it with her relaxed lips. That drove Pia wild. And Marika grew hot and excited all over again as the inarticulate cries, halfway between moans and entreaties, rang in her ears.

It was an hour and a half before they were finally dressed and descending in the hotel lift. They decided to have breakfast in one of the cafés which lined the Champs-Elysées before going shopping.

Sitting outside on white wrought-iron chairs, they watched the tourists and native Parisians going about their business. As Marika bit into a *pain au chocolat*, she experienced a pang of perfect happiness.

Although she knew that a mountain of work awaited her back at the PrimeLight offices in London's Docklands, she was content to live just for the moment.

She looked forward to browsing around the glassed-over shops of the *galéries* with Pia and then returning to their hotel in the late afternoon. They would make love on the fabulous king-size bed, with the golden light of the afternoon sun streaming in through the windows, the patterns from the cast-iron window casings making fantastic prints on their naked bodies.

Later they'd change and go out to enjoy the Paris night life. And then there was the long, velvet-darkness of the night to look forward to.

Even though Pia had brought her to orgasm twice already that morning, the remembered pleasure sent a sweet ache to throb between Marika's thighs. She uncrossed her legs, feeling how hot and swollen she was under the skimpy lace bodysuit. The silk crotch that fastened between her legs with poppers was damp from her intimate moisture.

The half cups of the bodysuit allowed her breasts to bulge into a deep cleavage. She liked the feeling of the cream lace as it rubbed gently against her prominent nipples when she moved. Over the bodysuit she wore a cream satin suspender belt and sheer pale stockings. A stylish linen dress, knee-skimming and styled in military fashion, showed off her long slim legs. Pale kid leather sling-backs completed her outfit.

Under a long white linen jacket, Pia wore one of

her simple, unstructured shift dresses. This morning it was long-sleeved and made of palest green raw silk. Her legs were encased in lacy tights and she wore wedge sandals so high that Marika wondered how she walked in them. When Marika commented, Pia laughed and told her that one of the top models had taken a tumble on the Paris catwalk when wearing similar shoes.

'The photographers loved it,' she said, dipping a corner of her croissant into her dish-like cup of creamy coffee. 'She probably did it on purpose to get extra press coverage!'

Marika was conscious of the many admiring glances that came their way. She knew that they presented an attractive, even enigmatic, picture. The sophisticated Englishwoman, cool and well-groomed, and the flamboyant young model, who, despite her sensuality, possessed a fresh, dreamy innocence.

She sat back in her chair and took a long leisurely glance down the tree-lined Champs-Elysées. It seemed incredible that her life had changed so much in a few short weeks. Impossible now to imagine how she had existed without the excitement and the challenge of belonging to the Discipline of Pearls.

I'm blessed, she told herself. Perhaps it is possible to have everything you want. To live a double-life and to enjoy both gleaming facets of it.

As she bent forward, the pendant she wore between her breasts moved. The weight of it, warm from her skin, was a constant reminder of her secret. Now she wore the entwined hearts – who knew what else there was to gain? And what privileges she might expect?

* * *

Marika arrived back at her Primrose Hill flat late on Sunday night.

She dumped the carriers with her Paris purchases in the kitchen, then rewound the tape on her answerphone. There were two messages from girlfriends she hadn't seen for months, suggesting that they have lunch sometime. She smiled to herself. The news about the split-up with James had travelled fast. There was no shortage of shoulders to cry on – if she needed them.

James had called four times over the weekend, each message slightly more frantic than the last. She felt irritated that he was hanging on. This behaviour wasn't like him. She had always thought him so strong and decisive. Why didn't he believe her when she told him it was over?

As she listened to the final message from James she felt herself come back down to earth with a crash. Her pleasure in the Paris trip dissolved. James sounded so crushed, almost tearful.

He said that he was desperate to see her. They must talk. He'd come to a decision. He was going to leave his wife and move into Marika's flat with her.

'Oh no. He wouldn't!' she groaned aloud. 'He couldn't be that stupid. Surely.'

Horrified at the prospect of him arriving at the door, cases in hand, she telephoned him at once. It was after midnight, but she knew that he'd be awake.

'Marika! Thank God you've phoned. I've been going out of my mind. I was on the point of coming round.'

'I've been away. A business trip to Paris. It's not unknown, is it? There was no need to panic.'

'No. Of course not. Sorry. I'm so glad you rang. Shall I come over now? You got my message . . .'

'No. Don't come over,' she said. Why must he make this so difficult? Never once in all the years she'd known him had he even *thought* of leaving his wife.

Hardening her voice she told him in no uncertain terms that if he wanted to leave his wife that was up to him, but she wanted no part of it.

'But I thought you'd be pleased. Isn't that what you wanted?' He sounded bemused.

'It might have been once. But that was a long time ago, back at the beginning. I meant it when I said we were finished. It wasn't some elaborate ruse to force your hand. Stay with Anthea, James. You're well suited. It would be cruel to hurt her needlessly. She doesn't know about us. Why tell her now that it's over?'

'Then . . . you really don't want me?'

She drew a deep breath, knowing that she had to be cruel.

'No, James. I don't. I'm happy without you. I want to live my life. And I'm afraid that you're just not a part of it anymore.'

She heard his indrawn breath and imagined his blue eyes widening in shock.

'You selfish bitch! You bloody little cow! After all I've done—'

Marika put the phone down. Her hands were shaking, but she felt a sense of finality. Now that James was angry he'd start getting over her. It was best that he blamed her for the break-up. She knew that she wouldn't be hearing from him again.

As she waited for the kettle to boil she took the black card out of her handbag. It was the card Stone had given her, back at the club in Paris. She laid it next to the phone, a tiny smile curving her lips as she wondered how long she could hold out before she dialled that raised gold number and set off for another assignment.

Marika slept well. She slept well every night now. Her mind was clear and sharp and there was no sign of the restlessness, the sense of emptiness she had experienced a few weeks back.

Her body gave back the slight tingle of perfect health as she showered and dressed. She wished that she could phone Pia and wish her good morning, but the model had gone straight from Paris to Milan. They had parted at the airport, not caring who saw them embrace.

Pia had a tight schedule of photographic fashion shoots for magazines, portrait shots for an American make-up company, and catwalk work for Italian designers. It would be weeks before she was available.

'When I get back we'll take a holiday together. Perhaps the Bahamas. I have a friend with a yacht,' Pia said.

Marika was missing her new friend already. As she drove to the office, she comforted herself with the knowledge that Pia was as enchanted by the intensity and heat of their new relationship as she was herself.

Gwen looked up and smiled as Marika strolled past her desk.

'Hope you're well rested,' Gwen grinned. 'Coffee before work?'

'Mmmm. Please. I'll take the appointments

book in now. Might as well see what's in for me.'

She scanned the pages. No shortage of people needing image-building, she thought. But the heavy schedule of work did not dismay her.

She set to with a will, drawing up a rough plan for a party for a prestigious French fashion house who were launching their New Year theme called 'Season of the Moon'. Ironically the party was to be situated at Panton, outside Paris, at the company's new workshop.

Marika was so engrossed in the party arrangements that she worked well past her usual lunchtime, causing Gwen to comment,

'Well. I don't know what you did over the weekend, but I think you should bottle it and give me some!'

Marika laughed. She couldn't quite imagine stoic, dependable Gwen getting involved in the jewelled world of her secret persona.

'Oh Gwen, would you make a note that I'm booking myself out of the office for two weeks in June?'

Gwen raised her eyebrows.

'You haven't had a holiday in over a year. It's long overdue if you ask me. Going somewhere nice?'

Marika smiled brilliantly. 'Probably cruising around the Bahamas in a yacht.'

Gwen's face was a picture. 'Well, that's certainly the way to get over a broken love affair!'

Marika felt like giggling like a teenager. Somehow she suppressed the urge. That would *really* have unsettled Gwen. When her personal assistant had gone back to her desk, Marika opened her handbag and took out the black card.

The embossed gold telephone number occupied

her thoughts at all times. It was never the same number twice. She enjoyed the anticipation of thinking about phoning, hearing Stone's voice – or would it be a stranger again?

She knew that she was playing a game with herself. It was like holding back an orgasm, letting the excitement fade, only to rise again to a higher, sweeter pitch. She enjoyed having a secret. It was the best thing in the world to have her memories, to take them out to savour whenever she wished.

Back at the flat she masturbated three nights in a row, deliberately taking the edge off her simmering sensuality. She used her vibrator in a slow, leisurely way; feeding her hunger as much as assuaging it. She bought herself new underwear, skimpy and daring items of shiny, black stretch Lycra; G-strings of black lace, and a real corset with laces, like the one she'd worn in the club in Paris.

Remembering something Stone had said about black leather suiting her, she began to notice clothing she would never have thought of buying before. Taking an extended lunch hour, she went to Soho and found a shop that sold the sort of items she was looking for; elbow-length gloves, rubber stockings, buckled waist cinchers, all the classier items jumbled together with garish plastic sex aids.

Hanging in her wardrobe now was a selection of expensive and beautifully-made leather and latex accessories. Just putting them on, parading in front of the mirror in her flat, gave her a sense of pleasure and pride in the way she looked. She knew that she'd get the chance to wear her new clothes soon. All it took was one phone call.

By the end of the week Marika was so sexually

charged that she could think of nothing else but hands on her body, a mouth against hers, rigid sex-flesh thrusting into her willing body. She thought her state must be obvious to anyone who studied her closely and was amazed that no one seemed to notice anything different about her.

She left the office on Friday, her blood fairly singing with the knowledge that she could hold out no longer. It was an effort to drive home carefully, but she managed it by forcing herself to concentrate. She registered the other traffic only as streams of lights reflected in the wet tarmac of the roads and reached home with no memory of the route she'd taken.

Garaging the BMW she hurried into the flat. Dumping her handbag on the hall floor, she picked up the phone before she'd even taken off her jacket.

On the third ring, Stone answered the phone.

'Did you enjoy Paris?' he said, without waiting for her to speak. 'I found your performance with Pia utterly enchanting.'

'I enjoyed myself immensely,' she said with feeling. 'Even your desertion couldn't spoil it for me. In fact, I think you'd have been in the way.'

There was a barely perceptible pause. She knew that she'd wounded him. Good. A little flare of satisfaction warmed her skin.

Stone laughed. He was trying to sound unmoved, but she thought his laughter had a hollow sound.

'How quickly the fledgling tries its wings,' he said dryly. 'You've earned yourself the inter-twined heart and now you grow bold. That's to be expected and encouraged, but don't reach too high, too soon, Marika. Bide your time and the rewards will be great.'

'I've had enough of you telling me what to do!' she snapped. 'Your bloody veiled threats and promises. Why don't you tell me all this face to face? What are you afraid of? Do you think you might like it too much if we were to establish a relationship?'

'Well, well. You are perceptive. Show your claws if it pleases you. I've got a thick skin. I'd like nothing better than to come to you, to sheath myself in you, so that you retract those claws and start to purr a little. But it's not yet time for us to meet as man and woman. You still have to serve your apprenticeship. Now. Are you ready for your next assignment?'

'Yes,' she said, shaken by the eroticism of his words and the intensity of his voice. 'Yes. I'm ready.' She was unable to keep the longing out of her voice and knew that he'd perceive it.

Stone laughed again; this time she heard the note of satisfaction.

'Then go to this address. Be there at midnight. Your contact will be waiting for you. Be gentle, Marika.'

She recognised the address of a run-down area on the outskirts of London. There was nothing there but deserted warehouses and the shell of an industrial development which was never completed because of lack of funds.

She was about to protest, to ask if he was sure that she should go there, but Stone had rung off. As she replaced the phone, she replayed his final words in her head.

'Your contact will be waiting for you. Be gentle.'

Damn Stone. He'd done it again. This latest

assignment was as intriguing and challenging as anything she'd experienced so far. And he knew that she would meet it willingly.

CHAPTER

9

Marika headed out of London on the Westway, through Acton and Ealing, and drove for half an hour before she reached the slip road which led to the partially built industrial estate.

As the BMW cruised over the bumpy road she saw the debris lying in shadowy piles all over the area. Most of the windows had been smashed in the warehouses she passed and a bright splash of graffiti adorned the blank face of one wall.

The address Stone had given her was easy to find. One road sign remained to give some focus to the sprawl of urban decay. She headed down Blakeford Drive and swung the car into a cul de sac, pulling up in front of a solid-looking warehouse.

She got out of the car and locked it, looking around for any signs of life. In central London a place like this would be a haven for squatters and the various people who lived on the streets. But out here, there were no bonfires in empty oil drums and no winos and drug users huddling together for warmth and company.

The whole place had a neglected and forlorn

air to it. It was quiet, the noise of traffic from the main road muffled by the tall, red brick walls that formed three sides of the square. The warehouse looked Victorian. It was built from red bricks, the large deep-orange kind, although they looked darker in the moonlight. There was a tower at one end of the building and a faded name, picked out in white stone, was still visible on the front façade.

Crunching over broken glass Marika entered the warehouse by a door that swung crazily from its hinges. Although she knew that she was expected and there was nothing to fear, prickles ran up and down her spine.

In the great, square vault of the empty warehouse it was easy to imagine that eyes were watching her. Bricks, girders and smashed glass littered the floor, hampering her path. She glanced up towards the topmost windows, where she was able to see the ceiling joists, the floors and ceilings of storerooms having fallen in long since.

It was that debris which cluttered the floor and made progress difficult if not dangerous. There was a musty, damp smell to the place. While she was deliberating whether to chance exploring the ruin, a movement in the shadows caught her eye. She turned towards it.

'Who's there?' she said, her voice firm and strong. 'I know there's someone over there. Come out. Show yourself.'

No one answered. She peered into the dusty darkness, the only illumination coming from the moonlight which streamed in through the panes of the blind windows. Marika tensed, her ears pricked to catch the slightest sound.

For a moment longer there was silence, then she heard a rustling as a shoe scraped through brick dust. A hand seemed to squeeze her heart and the breath dried in her throat. What if she had made a mistake and surprised an old derelict?

Then she heard more footsteps and someone stepped directly into a shaft of silver moonlight.

'Have you come here for me?' The voice was masculine, deep and soft. There was a note of longing there too.

That was something Marika understood. She smiled with relief. She ought to have known that anything orchestrated by the secret society would be perfectly safe – challenging certainly, and scary, but not downright dangerous.

The young man was tall and slim. He had light-coloured shoulder-length hair, straight and falling forward to brush the sides of his face. He wore a dark T-shirt under a leather jacket and black jeans tucked into studded and buckled biker boots.

'Come closer,' Marika said evenly.

Obediently the young man walked towards her. She saw that his face was strong-featured, but sensitive. Straight dark brows were drawn together above deep-set dark eyes. His nose was a trifle over-long, but his mouth more than made up for that slight fault. His lips were as finely chiselled as a woman's, full and soft and very kissable.

Marika's pulses quickened, but it wasn't fear she felt now. She was aware of a hot churning excitement in her belly. This time the situation was different. In all other encounters she had been the one who was the novice. Now the tables seemed to have been turned.

She smiled to reassure the young man. In some ways he reminded her of Pia, certainly he was striking enough to be a model for *GQ* magazine. She wondered what he did for a living. The almost feminine beauty of his face contrasted strongly with his broad shoulders and the clean, masculine lines of the rest of his body. Marika judged him to be about nineteen or twenty.

'What's your name?' she asked coolly, knowing instinctively that, in this encounter, it was *she* who was in complete control.

'Rafael . . . Rafael March,' the young man said, hesitantly. 'I . . . I was given this address and told to wait for someone. I was told that whoever arrived would . . . take care of me.'

'I see. Hold out your hands please.'

'But why? What for? I don't . . .'

'Just do it, please. Then I will explain everything.'

Slowly Rafael held out his hands. On the little finger of his left hand, as Marika had known there would be, was a ring. An oval of jet surrounded by tiny pearls. The jet was unmarked by any carving.

She felt a surge of elation. She knew it. He was a rookie, a fledgling, whatever the term was for a newcomer to the society. It seemed that she had been given the task of initiating him.

'When were you given the ring?' she asked.

'A week ago,' he said.

She grinned. 'It took you that long to phone the number on the black card? I only lasted two days.'

Rafael smiled for the first time, his lips curving in a conspiratorial smile. She saw that he had a gap in his front teeth. She liked it. It made him slightly less perfect and more human.

'You too?' he said.

She nodded. 'Women are given a pendant. You are a lucky young man. Only certain people are chosen to belong to this society. You won't have heard of the Discipline of Pearls. It will become very important to you. It has become so to me. But enough about that.' She paused and looked deeply into his eyes, letting him see what was there, then she tossed back her loose blonde hair.

'Talk can wait until later,' she murmured. 'Until – after.'

She let the word hang in the air between them. The shift in power, the role reversal, had made her bold. And she had been anticipating this meeting for over a week, a week of teasing herself to a fever pitch of sexual wanting.

Rafael watched her, his arms at his sides, a look of respect and fascination on his handsome face. He swallowed and she imagined that she could smell his nervousness. His dark eyes gleamed as they took in every detail of her body.

Marika lifted her chin and let him look. She knew that she looked good. Her high-necked black dress, worn over rubber stockings was short and tight. Her leather boots were laced up to the knee and under a short leather jacket she wore elbow-length leather gloves.

She smiled slowly. 'So Rafael. What shall I do with you?'

Holding her gaze he sank slowly to his knees, not caring about the dust and debris. As he looked up at her, she saw the desire and anguish on his face. And she knew that he was as starved for sexual release as she was.

In a daze of lust she looked at his upturned face, the erotic possibilities crowding her mind and making her shudder with anticipation. How should they begin?

Then Rafael made the decision for both of them.

'Please,' he whispered hoarsely. 'Do whatever you want with me. Make me your slave. Only for God's sake, let me serve you.'

For a moment longer, she hesitated. It was strange to think that she could order this beautiful young man to do anything she liked; stranger still to know that he would obey her implicitly. The novelty of having such power over a willing male flooded her with a new and powerful excitement.

'Go over there, to that wooden bench and take your clothes off,' she said softly.

Rafael picked his way across the littered floor, his heavy biker boots crushing the rotten wood and splintering glass under foot. Marika followed him, her high heels forcing her to go more slowly.

The wooden bench she'd spotted was the only piece of unbroken furniture in the place. It stood alone in the sea of debris, against a backdrop of flaking plaster. The bench was placed directly under a skylight, the moonlight pouring down onto it. Rafael sat down to pull his boots off, the silver light bleaching his light-coloured hair.

Marika watched him, her eyes half-closed with concentration. Rafael dropped his leather jacket to the floor and lifted the T-shirt over his head. His hands moved to the belt which held up his jeans.

'Wait,' she ordered.

Moving close, she ran her palms up the outsides of his arms, savouring the smoothness of his skin. His body hair was sparse and fair. She moved her hands inwards across his broad chest to brush lightly across the pronounced bulge of his pectorals.

Rafael's upper body was strong and muscular,

without being heavy. He looked as if he worked out in a gym or did some kind of manual work. Although broad at the shoulders, his body sloped to a neat, tight waist. His stomach was flat and marked by ridges of muscle.

Playfully Marika pinched his bronze male nipples. She smiled when he gasped and let his head fall back. For a moment longer, she toyed with the hard little pips. When he reached for her, she stood back.

'Drop your jeans,' she said.

Holding eye contact with her, Rafael unzipped his jeans and drew them down over his slim hips. Underneath he wore a tightly-fitting black posing pouch. The stretchy fabric was full to bursting, hardly able to contain his straining cock.

Marika reached out and trailed a finger across the bulge, then opened her hand and cupped the fabric pouch. He was hot and heavy in her hand. His balls were big and his cock thick and sturdy – just the way she liked her men.

Little tremors passed over Rafael's skin as Marika massaged his covered cock. The head pressed against the top of the pouch, where it met his belly, tenting the stretchy black fabric as it tried to escape. She could see the pronounced ridge of his glans and flicked it lightly with her thumbnail.

Rafael arched his back as she stroked, biting his lip as he tried to contain himself. His breath whistled between his teeth when she reached between his legs and caressed the firm pad behind his scrotum. Lifting the thong of fabric which rested between his buttocks, she curled her finger into the moist hairy crevice and pressed the pad of her finger against his anus.

Rafael's eyes widened at this intrusion, but he made no sound.

'Spread your legs,' she ordered, pressing harder so that the tip of one perfectly manicured nail slipped into his body.

Rafael did as she asked and she continued her intimate explorations, enjoying his confusion and mounting shame. His head was bowed and the long straight hair veiled his expression, but she knew that his cheeks were on fire.

'That will do for now,' she said at length, removing the very tip of her finger from his tight orifice. How powerful yet quiescent he was, an absolute delight.

'Shall . . . shall I take this off now . . .?' Rafael stuttered, looping his thumbs into the thongs which sloped upwards at either side of his groin.

Marika nodded. It would give him a moment to calm down. His balls had tightened as she stroked him and probed at the creased little orifice and she knew that he was aching to come.

'You'd better uncover yourself completely,' she said. 'I'd like to examine you properly before I decide whether I'll grant you release.'

Rafael's dark eyes opened wide as he absorbed the possibility that she might find him wanting. No doubt his beauty had been a passport for him in the past. Well, she wanted to make sure that he remained aware of the fact that he was a newcomer to the society, so far untried and unaccepted.

Rafael lifted the pouch free of his cock and lowered the scrap of fabric slowly. His cock sprang free, nudging against his stomach. Marika smiled and licked her lips.

He had a beautiful cock, not too long, but thick

and with a flaring tip. The glans was only partly covered by the foreskin and she could see the moist purplish skin with the slitted mouth in its centre. His shaft reared up from a cluster of light brown curls at his groin and his sac was firm and dark in colour.

She imagined how it would feel to have him push his cock into her, the hot flesh forging new pathways of sensation inside her. How delicious to imagine that thickened end surging against her womb.

She swept her eyes down the length of his body. God, he was beautiful. I must have done something good in my life to deserve this, she thought. Rafael's eyes met hers and she saw the confidence on his face. He had noticed how she looked at him and his mouth curved in a smile of pride.

He thinks he's irresistible, she thought. And immediately she wanted to teach him a lesson in humility.

'Show me how you make yourself come,' she said to him.

'What?'

She saw the heat rush into his face as he gazed at her with disbelief. She held his gaze. Ah, you didn't expect that, did you?

'You heard me, Rafael. Do it to yourself, while I watch you.'

'I don't think I can. I've . . . I've never done it . . . in front of anyone . . .'

'There's a first time for everything. Come on now. Show me how you masturbate. What about your promise to obey me?'

Slowly he brought his hand up and curled his fingers around his shaft. He began stroking himself gently at first, the loose foreskin smoothing back from the big glans. As he became less self-conscious he pulled at himself more vigorously.

'I'll just make myself comfortable. You carry on,' Marika said.

She sat down on the bench, swinging her legs apart so that she straddled the wooden seat. Rafael's eyes fixed on her crotch where her short skirt had ridden up to expose the white flesh at the top of her rubber stockings. His eyes bulged as she trailed her hand between her legs and brushed her fingers against the triangle of lacy fabric which covered her sex.

Marika smiled slowly, opening her legs more widely as Rafael pumped energetically at his now hugely erect cock. It was almost purple in colour, the bulbous glans uncovered fully, gleaming and moist with clear juice.

'That's it Rafael. Work that shaft,' she said, the crude words exciting her as much as the sight of him. 'I want to see you spurt and then you're going to lick and suck me until I come. Would you like to feel me quivering and spasming against your mouth? Do you want to taste my pussy?'

'Oh yes. Oh God,' Rafael moaned, the cords in his neck standing out as he gave himself three final hard strokes.

His body tensed and jets of creamy semen shot into the air and spattered the dusty floor. Rafael cried out in triumph, both hands clamped to his pulsing groin.

Marika felt her insides dissolve and a warm trickle of juice press against her labia as she watched his expression; the almost dreamy look of pleasure-pain, the open mouth, and the dark, unfocussed eyes. He looked so beautiful when he came, like a suffering saint in a religious painting. El Greco, she decided. Rafael had the pale, elongated features of one of that painter's subjects.

The crotch of her G-string was soaked. As she moved, the swollen folds of her sex slipped against each other. She knew that she'd come from the slightest touch. But she wanted to make this last.

'Come here,' she said to Rafael, whose cock was still glistening with the final silky drops. 'Sit on the bench, between my legs.'

He did as she ordered, reaching out almost reverently to pick up each of her feet in turn and to kiss the pointed toe of each shoe. Then he ran his hands up her rubber-encased calves and moved up to the bare flesh above her stocking tops.

Without being told to, he bent forward and mouthed the tender skin of each inner thigh. Marika surged against his warm lips. The touch was exquisite. She felt him nuzzling more deeply into her crotch, worshipping and exploring with each new caress.

Rafael's hands followed the path his mouth had taken. His thumbs pressed on the flesh to either side of the lace-covered triangle, opening the slit of her sex. The lace of her G-string scraped deliciously against her swollen clit and she moaned, wanting more, wanting everything he would do to her.

Then, as Rafael continued kissing her aching mound, he slipped his thumbs under the edges of the lace fabric, easing it away from her sex. His thumbs ran up the parted lips of her sex, peeling them back and then smoothing them together.

The referred pressure on her clit caused it to throb and swell even more.

Marika took her weight on her elbows, drew up her legs and let her knees fall apart, spreading herself like a feast before him. She was beyond telling him what to do, all her concentration was centred on the pulsing spot between her legs and the gathering tension in her belly.

But Rafael needed no urging, no direction. Sliding one hand under her buttocks he lifted her slightly, so that he could pull the G-string free. The scrap of lace and elastic was caught like a narrow bridge between her thighs. She adjusted one leg so that he could remove it.

'God. You're wonderful,' Raphael breathed as he gazed on her uncovered sex.

He pushed her short skirt up to her waist, exposing her rubber belt and suspenders. With a groan he bent his head and began kissing her pubic mound, nuzzling the silky brown fleece. Marika allowed her head to fall back, her mouth opening on a moan of pleasure as his hot tongue drove into her.

She worked herself back and forth on his tongue, which was spearing her like a tiny cock. Rafael drew back for a moment, then began to lick her, exploring the wet, musky folds with long, loving strokes.

Marika arched her back, uttering guttural little cries, her legs waving wildly in the air as the tension inside her built, crested, exploded into a mind-numbing orgasm. All the longing of the past week coalesced into the wild sensations which were coursing through her.

She collaped onto her back as the pleasure began to fade, her hands stretching out to caress

Rafael's tumbling hair. He lay with his cheek against her belly, resting on the strip of rubber which encircled her from waist to hip.

It was some time before she stirred and opened her eyes. The great empty vault of the warehouse soared overhead. And, suddenly, she couldn't bear the desolation of the place. She wanted to lie with Rafael in some place of comfort, to kiss him back to a state of urgency and to draw all that frenzied male hardness into her body.

Rafael raised his head and smiled at her.

'What do we do now?' he said, casually. 'Go our separate ways?'

'Is that what you'd like to do?'

'God no,' he said. 'But I didn't know whether you'd want . . . I don't know what the rules are.'

'I do,' she smiled warmly. 'The rules are mine to change. Get dressed. You're coming with me.'

'Right on!'

Flashing her a look of delight, Rafael got to his feet. Holding out a hand to her, he helped her up. His mobile lips parted in a grin, showing the gap in his teeth.

'In that case, your place or mine?' he said.

Marika laughed with pure enjoyment. He was so vital suddenly, his face alight with joy.

'Oh, I think your place, this time. Don't you?'

Marika swung the BMW around a bend, following Rafael's Harley-Davidson as it purred through the London streets. She could see him sitting upright on the motorbike, not hunched forward as he would be if he was riding a less classy machine. The light from street-lamps washed over his black leathers and threw glints from his oval-shaped crash helmet.

He looked like a night creature, at one with the gleaming black and chrome machine. She was reminded of the attenuated limbs and the smooth, black shiny skull of the monster from Ridley Scott's *Alien* film.

Rafael drew the Harley to a halt in front of a pair of huge wooden gates screened by a diamond-patterned metal grill. The gates had been set into an archway of red brick. Other archways led off to the left and right. Overhead she could see the dark mass of the old railway bridge, a straight mark against the indigo skyline.

Rafael came over to her and she slid the car window down.

'I'll unlock the gates. You can put the car inside. It's not a good idea to leave it outside in this neighbourhood.'

He unlocked the security gate and slid it open, then dispensed with a padlock. The huge wooden doors swung open and Marika drove the BMW into the space inside.

As she got out of the car, the smells of oil and chrome polish filled her nostrils. Rafael parked his Harley, then locked the wooden gates behind them.

She glanced around. The space under the archway was huge. A line of gleaming motorbikes stood off to one side, their chrome engines, mirrors and coloured frames as near to perfection as was possible in any inanimate object.

Marika wasn't 'in' to motorbikes, but she could appreciate the singular beauty of these machines. Some of them were embellished with artwork. A green-haired siren decorated the petrol tank of one. Gold snakes were entwined around the extended front forks of another.

'My speciality,' Rafael said, coming up behind her and encircling her waist. 'I buy and sell Harleys. I do the paint jobs myself.'

He nuzzled into her neck and she felt his lips brushing the sensitive area at her nape.

'Mmmm. You smell great,' he said. 'And I can still taste your pussy on my mouth.'

She turned into him and wound her arms around his neck. His uncertainty back at the warehouse had gone. She liked this side of him. On his own ground he was relaxed, slightly brash. They kissed, Rafael's tongue probing deeply into her mouth.

It was as if her tongue was connected directly to her sex. Little flickers of heat licked out from her swelling clit. When she pulled away her breath was coming fast.

'Didn't we have unfinished business?' she whispered against his mouth.

'So we did,' he grinned crookedly. 'Follow me. My flat's upstairs.'

He led her to a metal staircase at the back of the building. She walked up the stairs in front of him, conscious that his eyes were glued to her swaying rear. The stairs emerged through a square sky-light directly into a room.

His flat ran the length of the archway. The long, low room had been constructed by adding a wooden floor above the garage-showroom below. The original brick arch forming the ceiling had been painted white and a semi-circular window, floor-length and uncurtained, let in light at either end of the flat.

She glanced around. The room was sparsely furnished and immaculate. Two chairs made from old leather car seats and chrome tubing stood either side of a black lacquer table. Shiny black pots held palms, and narrow slatted blinds set into free-standing wooden frames divided the single room into living and sleeping areas.

The black and white decor, the sense of light and space, had a Japanese feel to it. Three paintings side by side hung on one wall. Each was an air-brushed painting of a Harley-Davidson.

'Did you do those?'

Rafael nodded. 'The blue one's my favourite. It's an Electroglide.'

Marika was impressed and didn't trouble to hide the fact. The paintings were excellent and the room looked like something out of *House and Garden* magazine.

She knew now that she had been right about the sensitivity of his face. Those moody dark eyes and that chiselled mouth bore the mark of someone who needed to express himself through works of art. And his hands. They were square, capable of stripping down a motorbike engine, but the fingers were slim and long.

Fingers that had coaxed the pleasure out of her body, stroked her sex and pressed against her throbbing bud. She shuddered remembering . . .

'You like my place?'

She nodded, dragging her attention back to what he was saying. 'Oh yes. It's great. Really stylish.'

'Not the pit you'd expected? When I tell people that I live over my garage, they expect it to be like a storeroom, all junk and grease.'

How many girls have you brought up here to show them that they were wrong, she thought. Then dismissed it. She didn't care. The only reality for them was here and now. Whatever either of them did was immaterial. In the Discipline of Pearls they came together in a unique and singular relationship.

'Come here,' she said.

Rafael's eyes darkened with longing. She saw a muscle twitch in his cheek.

She reached for his hand and led him over to his bed. A patchwork leather cover was thrown over a mattress resting on a futon base. Rafael sat down and pulled her down with him. Together they rolled on the bed, their hunger for each other rising and blotting out all need for further small-talk.

'Do it to me,' Marika said huskily. 'Don't be gentle. I'm ready for you.'

She tore at the zip on his jeans, reaching inside and pulling his cock free. He was hard and ready. She stroked him, loving the weight and heat of him. The tip of his cock was weeping a slick, salty fluid. She captured it on the ball of her thumb and rubbed it around the slit in his glans.

Groaning and pushing himself towards her hand, Rafael eased her thighs apart with his knee. With one hand he pushed her skirt up until it lay in a tight tube around her waist. Dragging the lace G-string down, he left it slung around one ankle.

Pushing her hands under his T-shirt Marika raked his strong young back lightly with her nails. He wriggled out of his jeans, managing to get them down to his knees before he remembered that he still had his boots on. He swore with impatience and began to lever himself away from her.

She wound her arms around his waist and pulled him back against her. It seemed the most important thing in the world at that moment, to retain the closeness between them. She couldn't bear to lose that bar of heat and strength that was pressing into her inner thigh.

'Leave them on,' Marika said. 'Put it in me, Rafael. Now. I can't wait.'

He needed no more urging. His hands shook as he slipped the condom onto his rigid flesh.

Marika kept her legs apart only slightly so that the channel of her sex was tight, though yielding. Rafael pushed into her, the bulbous head scraping deliciously past the closure of her flesh and only when he had slipped inside and filled her completely did she open her legs wide.

Wrapping her legs around his back, she rubbed against the base of his cock and he rode her hard. He slammed into her, taking her at her word. It was what she wanted, to lose herself completely in the frenzy of his passion.

His balls slapped against her upturned buttocks as his lubricated shaft plunged into her, knocking against her womb and driving her wild with lust. Her slippery walls were stretched to accommodate his bulk and she felt her entrance fluttering as his pubic hair grazed it on each inward thrust.

Rafael threw his head back and groaned loudly as he spilt himself inside her. She raked at his hard, tensed buttocks, grinding the firm little nub of her clit against the base of his belly. Her climax washed over her just as Rafael collapsed onto her, his hair swinging forward to lie across her cheek.

She held him tight, stroking his back and soothing him as if he was a child. He was wracked by after-tremors and kept kissing her mouth, tiny, bruising kisses of gratitude. She wasn't sure whether he was crying, but she felt pretty close to it herself.

After a while Rafael rolled away from her and dispensed with the condom. Wrapping the patchwork cover around them, he tucked her head into the crook of his arm.

Marika murmured with contentment and slipped one arm around his broad chest. In a few hours London would be awakening and her hold on normality would return.

But for now she was content to lie cocooned in the embrace of this beautiful boy. It occurred to her that she didn't know whether she was breaking any rules by coming back to Rafael's flat.

No doubt Stone would get to know of her actions. If he was displeased, she'd hear about it. As she closed her eyes and drifted off into sleep, she thought, I don't care if you do disapprove, Stone. It's your own fault for staying in the background.

Rafael was vital and warm, so much more alluring than her cold, remote mentor. But she knew that wasn't strictly true. Rafael was beautiful, Pia was too. But if Stone was to reach out for her, she'd go to him at once. And no questions asked.

On the borders of sleep, she didn't question the flash of insight. She gave a deep sigh and let her mind rove free.

That was just the way it was with Stone.

CHAPTER 10

Dawn was breaking as Marika drove back towards Primrose Hill. The sky looked exactly like slivers of smoked salmon lying on a silver dish.

She garaged the car and let herself into the flat. She felt wide awake and too active to sleep. Turning on the bath taps, she left the bath filling as she pulled off her clothes and threw them into a covered linen basket.

She washed her hair and wound a towel around her head. Sliding down so that her shoulders were under the hot perfumed water, Marika closed her eyes and let the events of the night replay themselves in her mind.

Strangely, it wasn't the sex that she remembered with the most clarity. She found that however much she enjoyed making love at the time, the pleasure itself was transitory. Probably that was why humans spent so much time and energy on the pursuit of pleasure. Who could actually recapture the precise feeling of an orgasm?

What she did remember was that Rafael had told her about Stone. For it was he who had given Rafael the pearl and jet ring.

It seemed that Rafael had a girlfriend whose father bred race horses. Occasionally he would stay at her house and they'd ride in the local woods.

'It was when I was returning to the house that a man on a black hunter rode up to me,' Rafael told Marika. 'It was Stone, I'm sure. From what you've told me about him, the description matches perfectly. Tall, thin, dark hair. He had a severe, handsome face and arresting dark eyes.'

She had nodded. 'Yes. That's him. What did he do?'

'Well, he just appeared on the track. It was a shock to have him galloping towards me, right out of nowhere. Francie, that's my girlfriend, had ridden off. We were racing back to the house. Anyway, I reined in, just managing to avoid crashing into Stone, almost unseating myself in the process. And Stone threw me this small box.'

'Did he say anything?' Marika asked.

'Just that I had been chosen for something special. And that it would be to my advantage to keep quiet about it for a while.'

'And you did?'

'Well, yes. I felt a bit foolish. How could I tell Francie that I'd almost been ridden down by a madman in the woods? Then, when I saw the ring – well, I was blown away by it. It must be worth a fortune. And the card, with the telephone number . . . It was like a special secret. I didn't want to tell anyone else. And now . . . Now that there's you . . .'

The rest of the conversation had faded as they kissed and began stroking each other again. They couldn't get enough of each other and had made love twice more before she had slipped out of the bed while he slept.

Rafael would see the note on the pillow when he awoke. She smiled as she recalled that he had made her promise to contact him, soon. She knew that she would do so. His telephone number was scribbled in her address book.

Between them Pia and Rafael had added a new dimension to her experience. Both of them were more than playthings, sensual beings who delighted her senses – it was true, but they were also people who fascinated her with their perception and talent and the uniqueness of their humanity.

If one of the rules of the secret society was that she was not to get involved with her partners after liaisons, then she was failing miserably.

Of course it would be impossible to start up any kind of relationship with everyone she was likely to meet through the society. But she couldn't help the fact that she was so drawn to Pia and Rafael.

It was almost as if the two of them had been chosen by Stone to seduce her, draw her in, and entrap her within the society. It hadn't occurred to her before that that was a distinct possibility. Stone knew a lot about her, too much. He probably realised that she was not naturally promiscuous and would soon lose interest in casual sexual encounters. For her, there had to be another element, something more tangible than the slaking of her sexual appetites.

Somehow though, she didn't think that it had been his intention for her to become attached to both Pia and Rafael. Or for them to also become obsessed with her.

As she squeezed a sponge and spread foaming bath oil over her limbs, she thought: what's done is done. However things turned out, Stone and the others – whoever they were – would just have to accept the fact that she did things her way.

While she was drying her hair, bending over so that the warm air would blow some lift into the roots, the post arrived. There was a postcard from Pia, a few bills, and a small, plain envelope. Turning the postcard over, she read it as she padded into the kitchen and switched on the kettle.

Pia sent her love and signed the card with an extravagant swirl. The bottom third of the card was a cross-hatch of kisses and underneath those, Pia had written in capitals, 'I MISS YOU, MADLY'.

Marika smiled, 'I miss you too, darling,' she said aloud.

She remembered the texture of Pia's warm olive skin and the smell of her hair. Probably Pia was lightly tanned by now and attracting even more attention from a string of Italian admirers.

Marika made coffee and sipped a cup while she opened the rest of her post. Wrinkling her nose at the bills, she put them aside. Slipping her finger under the flap of the small envelope, she eased it open.

Inside there was a single sheet of paper and a small black card with familiar gold lettering. She opened out the note and began to read.

'Since Rafael was not qualiied to give you your next assignment, I took the liberty upon myself. I trust that his – initiation was satisfactory for you both. I know that you went back to his flat with him. I understand that, though I do not approve. Rafael is a very tempting young man. I intend to sample him myself before too long. A word of warning. It is not wise to become too involved on a personal level with your fellow society members.'

She took a sip of coffee and then read on.

'The Discipline of Pearls is best thought of as something remote and separate from your everyday life. Mix up the two, and the mystery is lost. Only those of exceptionally strong character can manage to transform one sexual encounter into an ongoing relationship, let alone two. Why must you be so perverse? Isn't the sex and the thrill of the chase enough for you? You insist on behaving irrationally, Marika. You are the most troublesome of all my protégés. How annoying and yet how tantalising you are. Do you not realise how difficult it is to have regular lovers? It is almost impossible to remain pure and unsullied by petty jealousies and power struggles. Think carefully about this.'

It was signed, 'Stone'.

Marika read it through twice, then slammed it down onto the kitchen table. The bloody cheek of the man! All he ever did was give her advice. Never mind that she didn't ask for it, didn't want it.

Just who did he think he was anyway? He didn't know whether she was capable of seeing Pia and Rafael and feeling the same emotion for each of them. She didn't know whether it would work out either. But she demanded the right to try, to make her own mistakes without his damned interference.

Then she read between the lines and her mouth curved in a smile. So, he thought that it was a big mistake to become emotionally involved with other society members, did he? She had accused *him* of being afraid of precisely that, the last time she spoke to him on the phone. How ironic that he was furious with her for doing what he dared not do!

She laughed aloud. 'Oh, you're a coward, Stone. And I'm not. I'm brave and reckless. Maybe I'm a little foolish too, but I'm prepared to face my mistakes. But you, ah, you're missing out because you're so bloody terrified of committing yourself.'

Shoving the new black card into her bedside cabinet drawer, she dressed in a pair of seersucker trousers and pulled a red cotton cable sweater over them. Pulling on a pair of stout ankle boots and shrugging on her silk parka, she left the house.

She felt like walking down to Camden, where there were always bric-à-brac stalls lining the streets. Maybe she'd buy an old brooch to add to her collection of fun jewellery. Later she'd return one of those calls from her old girlfriends.

It would be good to chat over lunch and catch up on gossip. The letter from Stone had rattled her. Despite the fact that she was completely at ease with herself, he had a knack for making her doubt the wisdom of her actions.

She determined to push him to the farthest reaches of her mind. But the little black card nagged at her as usual. And this time, she knew that the card came directly from Stone.

Was the day when they would meet face to face getting nearer? She had preparations of her own to make.

Marika took Stone's letter with her to the office. It was the first time she'd gained any insight into his thoughts. Admittedly the 'conversation' was one-way, but she knew that the letter was a breakthrough.

Before now, he had given little of himself away. Their telephone conversations were short and infuriatingly obtuse. The letter was something different. She sensed his annoyance, his confusion. He called her 'perverse'. She smiled. Maybe he hadn't anticipated that side of her.

She knew the source of his anger, having sensed that he wasn't often wrong about people. Well no one can be right all the time, she thought.

She was getting under his skin. What a delightful concept. Way to go, as the Americans said.

She tried to picture Stone's face and was alarmed to find that she could only remember an amalgam of details, like a list. She knew his face was lean, with high cheekbones; his hair was dark and close-cropped, fitting like velvet or suede to his patrician skull; and his eyes were dark, their expression cool and implacable.

But the essence that was truly Stone eluded her. What was his smile like? What reflection did she see in his eyes when he looked at her? Strange how she could remember his smell, perfectly.

It had been weeks since that meeting in the underground car park. It felt more like a year. The only other time she had seen him, face to face, was through a haze of smoke in the Paris nightclub. The time when he had come to her in the hotel room in London didn't count. She hadn't seen him then, although she had felt him. She could recall his every touch and remember how it felt to have him thrusting inside her.

But his face – she was alarmed to think that she

couldn't see it clearly. And at a loss to understand the panic she felt because of that fact.

Marika completed her work at the office in her usual efficient manner. The days passed in a welter of phone calls, meetings, drinks parties. If Gwen noticed that she was distracted, she gave no sign of it.

Marika visited a printer's during a lunch hour and made a purchase. When she met Stone she'd be prepared.

One night she dressed in a striking emerald silk gown and pearl accessories and took a taxi to Annabel's. She was accompanying a client, an actor in a popular television soap, as he made an appearance at the top night-spot. After refusing his offer to come back to his house for a nightcap, she called him a cab and then took a separate one home. It was three a.m. before she fell into bed and she had an early start the next day.

The following morning she drove up to Liverpool, where she was to escort a well-known author to the Aintree race track. After the Grand National, Jake Somerville, an ex-jockey, was to sign copies of his bestselling thrillers.

The day went well. The race track was crowded with notables and celebrities and her client sold fifty books and signed many more. As Jake kissed her on the cheek and thanked her for her support, he slipped a wad of notes into her hand.

'What's that for?' she asked.

Jake grinned. He was an attractive man in his sixties. His thick, grey hair was brushed straight back from a broad forehead.

'That's your winnings, m' dear. I put a "pony" on for you and the beggar came in at ten to one.

You treat yourself, princess.'

Marika laughed and thanked him. Two hundred and fifty pounds was a sizeable tip. She normally didn't encourage clients to give her gifts, but Jake was an exception. He was a lovable rogue, completely incorrigible, and one of her favourite clients.

After a meal of roast beef with all the trimmings and crème brûlée to follow, which he insisted on paying for, she took her leave of Jake and drove back to london. She had time to think as she cruised down the motorway. However stimulating her lifestyle was, it was nothing in comparison to her exploits within the secret society.

When she got back to Primrose Hill it was late evening. She drove straight to her flat, showered, changed and then picked up the telephone.

A woman answered and gave her instructions to go to an address in Hampstead. The woman's voice had an upper-class twang. Rather bitchily, Marika imagined her wearing a waxed coat and green wellies.

She had really expected Stone to answer and her disappointment was marked. For a moment, she didn't concentrate on what the woman was saying.

'You're to dress in a summer frock. And wear pale stockings and high-heels, but no other underwear,' the woman said.

Marika thought of remonstrating with her, even refusing to do as she was asked, but she was curious. This was a different sort of liaison. No one had asked her to dress in a specific way before.

'You'll accept this commission?'

'Yes,' Marika said sulkily, and replaced the phone.

Sorting through her wardrobe restored her good humour. She found a white voile dress which seemed perfect for her needs. It had a softly draped bodice and a bias cut skirt, so that it floated around her calves as she walked. She fastened a peach satin suspender belt around her waist and pulled on a pair of sheer, silky stockings. White peep-toe sandals completed her outfit.

As instructed to, she left off her bra and slip. She did a twirl in front of her wardrobe. Whoever she was to meet ought to be satisfied. The shape of her breasts was clearly visible and the large, dark aerolae of her nipples pressed against the thin white cotton. The dress swished around her slim thighs as she descended the stairs.

Shrugging a car coat on over the dress, Marika left the flat, the now familiar feeling of excitement making her fingers tremble and causing her sex to grow hot and moist.

It didn't take long to drive to Hampstead. She headed for Chalk Farm and then on to Belsize Park. The address she had been given was to the west of Hampstead Heath. Navigating the side streets of Hampstead High Street, she swung the BMW around a bend and pulled up opposite a detached Victorian house.

The house was tall and narrow, with gothic arched windows and an ornate front porch. Opening the front gate she walked along a tiled path which was bordered by a clipped box hedge, and climbed the marble steps leading up to the front door.

A young woman in a maid's uniform opened

the front door. Marika stared at her in surprise. A frilled white cap topped her sleek brown curls and her black dress was short and full. A frilled white apron, too tiny to be practical, was tied around her waist. Her slim legs, exposed to mid-thigh, were encased in sheer black stockings.

The woman smiled, her generous lips parting to show perfect teeth.

'Please come in. You're expected,' she said, her eyes twinkling in a friendly way.

Marika returned the smile. She stepped into a spacious hall and waited for the woman to close the front door.

'May I take your coat? Thank you. Ah, you look perfect. The Major will be delighted. Would you come this way please? He's waiting for you in his study.'

Marika followed the 'maid' – for by now she had realised that the woman was playing a part, the same as she was. They went into the heart of the house. It smelt of lavender polish and the dusty warmth of age. Somewhere a clock struck ten-thirty, the strokes ringing out into the muffled silence of the house.

'Here we are. Go straight in.'

Marika walked into a large comfortable room. The walls were lined with book shelves. A large mahogany table of antique Spanish design was set in the centre of the room. Six matching chairs were placed around the table. Piles of books and magazines lay on the table top.

Three studded red-leather chairs were grouped around a fireplace. One of them was occupied by an elderly man. In the other sat a younger man, thick-set and expensively dressed in a cashmere sweater and light woollen trousers. As Marika entered the room, the elder of the two pushed himself to his feet and held out his hand.

'Ah, I'm very glad to meet you. Delighted in fact,' he smiled, pumping her hand with considerable strength. 'You are?'

'Marika.'

Marika smiled. The Major could have been any age from sixty to early seventies. He had obviously been a very handsome and vigorous man once, but age had honed down his large frame and added hollows to his thin cheeks. His hair was white and thick and fell to his shoulders. His eyes, though faded to the colour of stone-washed denim, were keen and sparkling with excitement.

'A lovely name,' the Major said. 'Well, let's get acquainted with each other, shall we? You've already met Lisa. This is Steven.'

The second man stood up and held out his hand. 'Charmed,' he said, his voice deep and well-modulated, with a European accent. His handshake was cool and firm. He held her hand for a fraction longer than was necessary, then let it go and sank into his chair.

Steven looked to be in his late thirties. He was only a little taller than she was and had very short, well-cut hair, which drew attention to his square jaw and strong features. His face was dominated by a sensual mouth. As his calm grey eyes flickered appreciatively over the softly draped bodice of her dress, Marika felt her nipples harden in response.

Turning to the 'maid', the Major said, 'Lisa will you bring us some wine? I think the malmsey on this occasion. Marika, will you sit opposite Steven and me? You'll feel the benefit of the fire there.'

Lisa bobbed a curtsy. After throwing Marika an eager little smile she left the room to fetch the wine. The Major seated himself and crossed his legs. Forming his fingers into a steeple-shape he pressed them against his mouth, his eyes studying Marika's face.

'I see that you dressed as I asked you to. Thank you. Now, I think a slight adjustment of your position, if you please. Raise your skirt, lift your legs and part your knees.'

Although Marika was becoming used to strange situations, the Major's words were still a shock. The resistance rose up in her, but Steven was looking at her so intently that she felt a frisson of excitement run down her back. Both he and the Major exuded an air of well-bred charm. She found herself drawn to them both.

'Certainly,' she said coolly, hoping that her nervousness did not show.

Suddenly she wanted to impress these cultured men, to show them that she was as accomplished and sophisticated as she imagined them both to be. She lifted her legs and placed her feet on her chair seat.

The heels of her white sandals made little dents in the padded red leather, but the Major didn't seem to mind that. Slowly she lifted up the floaty hem of her dress and bunched it up around her waist, then let her knees fall open.

'Ah. Delightful. Is she not, Steven?'

'Perfection,' Steven said, his voice sounding slightly hoarse.

The Major sighed and leaned back to enjoy the sight she presented. She felt only a slight prickle of shame as two pairs of eyes roved over her white thighs and exposed sex. The Major's expression was so rapt that she felt a strange kind of pride in being spread before him. Steven's reaction was altogether more carnal and Marika hardly dared to meet his eyes.

The door to the study opened and Lisa returned with a silver tray bearing a crystal decanter and glasses. Marika was overcome by self-consciousness; she shifted as if to change position and the Major held up his hand.

'Stay as you are, please. Isn't she a perfect subject, Steven? Perhaps you would like to examine the little treasure trove between her thighs?'

Steve smiled, a mere lifting of the corners of his sensual mouth. 'I'd like Lisa to perform that service for me.'

'An excellent idea,' the Major said. 'Would you, Lisa?'

'As you wish, gentlemen,' Lisa said, moving over to stand to one side of Marika's chair.

'If you will permit me,' she said, reaching between Marika's spread legs and laying gentle fingers on her sex.

The colour rose into Marika's cheeks as Lisa stroked and manipulated her expertly. It was one thing to sit opposite the two men while they looked her over, but quite another thing to have to subject herself to Lisa's ministrations and have them watch her responses.

The shame rose within her as she felt her sex begin to swell and grow damp. Her breasts burned under the thin cotton dress, her nipples gathering into throbbing little nubs. Steven's eyes darkened as he watched every delicate movement of Lisa's fingers. Her touch was featherlight, tantalising. With one fingertip she scooped up a drop of the pearly juice which was beginning to ooze from Marika's vagina and rubbed it onto her clit.

'That's enough for now,' the Major said. 'Will she do? Show me.'

Lisa turned towards him, rubbing two fingertips together as if assessing the silkiness of Marika's intimate moisture. She held out her fingers for Steven to examine too. Marika squirmed with mortification, while they discussed her amongst the three of them.

'Oh yes. She's wet already,' Steven said. 'She responds readily to stimulus. I think she'll be perfect for your purpose.'

'Good,' the Major said, turning to smile at Steven. 'I think we'll have a glass of wine first, shall we?'

Steven nodded, watching as Lisa poured the wine, then, in a normal conversational tone, he said to Marika, 'I'd like to see your breasts now. Uncover them, please.'

Swallowing hard and trying not to think of her state of arousal, and the visible evidence of it, Marika moved her hands to the front of her dress. The bodice had a cross-over front and she pulled the loose fabric aside, lifting her breasts free. Her breasts were supported and pushed upwards and inwards by the fabric bunched beneath them.

'Lovely,' the Major said. 'Don't you think so, Steven? And what do you think, Lisa?'

'Oh yes. Such nipples. They look so . . .'

'Inviting? Yes, don't they. Feel free, my dear. May as well prepare her thoroughly. Give her the wine first though. There's a danger that we'll forget it in the excitement and I won't see a good madeira wasted.'

He and Steven chuckled. Marika accepted a glass of the brown-red wine and sipped with relish. She noticed that the malmsey was the exact colour of her nipples.

Lisa knelt beside her chair and, leaning forward, took one of Marika's nipples into her mouth. She suckled noisily as Marika tried to concentrate on sipping the wine. She closed her eyes briefly. The sensation of the sweet, ticklish pulling, coupled with the taste of the strong, sweet wine, exerted a potent pull on her senses.

She knew that her sex was growing puffier, wetter, her vagina pulsing receptively, and was alarmed by the thought of the two men watching. She shifted on the leather chair, adjusting her legs, and felt the cotton skirt slip free of her bare buttocks. Now the spread-apart purse of her sex was pressing almost directly onto the warm red leather. With absolute horror she realised that soon she'd be dripping onto the chair seat.

'Excellent,' the Major said, as if he'd read her mind. 'I think you'd better stop that now, Lisa. We don't want to tire her too soon, do we?'

Lisa released the nipple she was sucking with reluctance. Pulling away, still attached for a second, she drew Marika's nipple out into a little tube shape. Marika barely suppressed a groan at the surge of prickly pleasure which darted straight to her groin.

She chanced a look at Steven and saw that one hand lay in his lap. He was moving his fingers gently, subtly over the straining front of his trousers. The thought of what lay under his hand made her tremble with anticipation.

Lisa rose to her feet, smiling down at Marika.

'Would you like some more wine? Are you quite comfortable?'

'Oh, er, yes,' Marika mumbled, answering both questions at once.

In fact, she was oddly at ease. The bizarre situation had its merits. Lisa was so solicitous, the Major's and Steven's manners impeccable. The relationship between them all, whatever that was, seemed to be one of mutual trust and liking. She sensed that they would not abuse her and was fascinated to see what part she was to play in the scenario they had engineered.

The room was warm and comfortable and she was feeling the effects of the wine. A pleasant glow seemed to have invaded her limbs, while the heat from the fire flickered over her uncovered thighs and lower belly.

Finishing his glass of wine, the Major rose to his feet.

'Get up now, if you please, Marika. I'd like to show you something.'

Marika stood up and her full skirt fell down to cover her to mid-calf. She pulled the loose front of her bodice to cover her breasts, acutely aware that her jutting nipples pressed wantonly against the thin fabric.

The Major pulled a number of books out of the book case and laid the chosen volumes on the polished table top. He waved her to a seat.

'These,' he said, his gesture encompassing the bookcases which lined the walls, 'are my pride and joy. The culmination of many years of collecting. I have many rare volumes. Would you care to look at some?'

Marika nodded, although she couldn't see what this had to do with her earlier experience at Lisa's hands. Then she looked at the first book and she realised that the Major did indeed have a rare collection. She had heard of some of the books, others were almost legendary in certain circles.

The Major had the most extensive collection of works of erotica she'd ever seen.

Steven had taken the seat next to her and was examining a book. She tried not to react to his proximity, but was acutely aware of his smell; expensive cologne, tobacco, and freshly-washed male.

She flipped over the pages of an illustrated edition of *Venus In Furs* and saw that it was a limited edition, dated nineteen twenty-eight. There was a biography of the life of Sacher-Masoch – a French work dated nineteen hundred and seven.

Her eyebrows rose as she saw that he possessed a first edition of *One hundred and twenty days of Sodom*.

The Major reached up to a top shelf and took down a large book. It was bound in the most exquisite pale leather and had lettering of gold-leaf on the spine. He held it out to her.

'This is the pride of my collection,' he said. 'The illustrations are all originals, all especially commissioned. Is it not beautiful? Feel the softness, the suppleness of the leather binding. It's priceless.'

Marika admired the book. It was indeed beautiful, the leather felt as soft as sueded silk. Inside it had marbled boards and end papers. She read the date – seventeen fifty-seven. Opening it she saw that the first illustrations were graphic in the extreme and skilfully executed. She sensed that this book was something to do with why she was there.

The Major beamed at her. 'Have you guessed? I can see that you are almost there. How clever of you. You're the first who has had any idea before they were told.'

He glanced across the table at Steven, who was sipping his wine and watching Marika's reactions.

'Shall I tell her, Steven? Or do you want that honour?'

Steven smiled. 'You tell her, Major,' he said. 'You are more experienced in these matters than I.'

'Very well. You see, Marika, today is the anniversary of a very special day – I'll explain more about that later. To mark the occasion I have arranged something for my pleasure and for the entertainment of my guest here. Steven is visiting for a few days only and I would like his stay to be memorable. Now, my dear, you can help me choose the precise nature of our pleasure. You strike me as a discerning young woman. So, turn the pages of this book until you find the illustration which you find the most stimulating. I want to know which picture speaks to you.'

He smiled at her, the creases around his faded eyes fanning out like rays. Marika returned his smile, aware that Steven was watching her every movement. He made her a little nervous. His heavy, considered silences were more disconcerting than his words.

'All right. I'll choose an illustration,' she said, beginning to turn the pages of the book.

It seemed then that this was not a unique occasion. There had been others before her, others who had leafed through this book looking for the portrayal of a scenario which appealed to them. And then they would re-create that scene, a living tableau for the Major's pleasure.

As she turned the pages, she felt her cheeks reddening. Every sexual act, every perversion was contained within this single volume. There were women making love to women, men with men, group sex, orgies, and every combination that was humanly possible. She was shocked by the detail of some of the illustrations, even while she admired the consummate artistry of their execution.

For a while she turned pages, until she had opened the book at its centre. She stopped, her pulses quickening at the scene which was portrayed by the double-page spread. It was so . . . kinky, so outrageous, so altogether fascinating that she couldn't stop looking at it.

'I approve of your choice,' Steven said at her shoulder, his voice holding a tremor of excitement.

'But . . . I haven't chosen yet,' she said.

He took the book from her and pushed it across the table towards the Major. 'Oh, but I think you have.'

Marika did not answer. For it was true. She *did* want to be at the centre of that particular erotic tableau, but she didn't know if she would have had the courage to decide that for herself. Steven's intervention had saved her having to admit to having such warped passions.

She hung her head a little as the Major and Steven studied the illustration. The details of it were imprinted on her thoughts. Part of her wanted to protest, to demand the right to choose something else, but her nerve endings were beginning to tingle with excitement. Oh, the awful lewdness of that drawing – the woman at the centre of the tableau was spread out on the table, while the man did *that* to her, and the others looking on were getting their own kicks copulating openly . . .

The Major made a sound of approval. 'This is a surprise. What a brave choice. You're an unusual young woman, Marika. Well now, it's obvious that Marika is to be at the centre of things. But which part do you wish to play, Steven?'

Marika held her breath, hoping that he would say what she wanted him to. Steven smiled and for the first time the smile reached his eyes. They looked like slate touched by the sun.

'Why not let Marika choose? Tell me – which character would *you* like me to play?'

Marika flushed to the roots of her hair. Both men and now Lisa, who had re-entered the room and was looking at the book, were waiting for her to reply. She was going to have to say it aloud. Lifting her chin, she locked gazes with Steven.

'I want you to be the one who does it to me. Who uses that . . . thing on me . . .' She tailed off, unable to bear their combined scrutiny, and his in particular, any longer.

'Well, my friend,' the Major breathed, 'I promised you something special to remember your stay by and Marika here will see that you get that.' He put the open book on a carved wood stand and propped it open. 'Now. Have you got everything we need, Lisa?'

'Almost, Major. I've just a few more preparations to make.'

Lisa had been clearing the mahogany table of books and magazines while they were talking. With deft movements, she put a pile of leather cushions and a leather cloth onto the polished table-top, along with a stoppered glass vial and an object which was wrapped in scarlet silk.

'If you please,' she gestured to Marika.

Marika's legs felt stiff. Now that the moment was here she felt a little afraid. How could she expose herself in front of all these people? It was surely impossible, but she found herself getting up onto the table and making herself comfortable by piling the cushions behind her.

'That's it,' Lisa said. 'Lift your dress, so that your bottom is resting on the leather cloth.'

Marika arranged herself so that she was in a sitting position with her bottom about a foot from the table's edge. She was told to let her legs fall apart and to place the soles of her feet together. This she did as best she could while still wearing the high-heeled sandals.

Lisa arranged Marika's dress, as she had done in the chair earlier. She lifted the filmy skirt and tucked it into a roll around Marika's waist. Steven stepped forward and slipped the cross-over top of the dress down Marika's arms a little way. Reaching inside the neckline, he grasped each breast in turn and eased it free.

Marika's breath quickened. Steven's cool, almost impersonal touch was very arousing. The way he lifted her breasts, arranging their fullness so that they were displayed to advantage, while the tightness of the fabric around her upper arms held her imprisoned, made her tingle with anticipation.

She glanced down at her body, shocked but fascinated by the spectacle of herself. Her breasts bulged lewdly, the dark crests of them gathered into prominent little stubs; the peach suspender belt was stretched smoothly across the slight mound of her belly and she could see the light brown tuft of her pubic hair between her widely spread thighs.

For a moment she was overcome by the very strangeness of her position. Here she was displayed on the polished table top, like some living erotic figurine. The open book was just feet away from her. If she glanced up she could see almost a mirror image of herself – except that the woman in the drawing had her head thrown back and her mouth stretched open in a rictus of ecstasy.

'Are you comfortable?' Lisa said, and the normality of the question penetrated Marika's consciousness.

'Yes, thank you,' she managed to say.

Lisa had the warmth and efficient manner of the best kind of nurse. She tried to think of that and not to dwell on the fact that the Major and Steven were watching her every movement. Then she felt Lisa's hands on her sex and as the sensations began to build into layers of pleasure, she forgot to think about anything else.

'Oh,' she gasped, as a warm trickle of something snaked down her clitoris and pooled in the depression of her vagina.

'It's just a special oil,' Lisa said. 'To get you ready for what Steven's about to do. You'll feel the effects of it in just a moment.'

And Marika did. Whatever was in the oil caused her to squirm and rub her bottom against the leather cloth. She felt as if the fleshy lips of her sex were swelling, burning, opening like the petals of some exotic flower caught by time-lapse photography.

'What's happening,' she moaned, as the wonderful warmth and heaviness spread inside her and set her womb throbbing and pulsing.

'It's just something to add to your pleasure,' Lisa whispered. 'Something to make you get all lovely and wet. Don't worry. The effects are short-lived and not harmful. I'll leave you in Steven's care now. The Major has need of me.'

Marika licked her dry lips. Thoughts of Spanish Fly entered her head, but she thrust them away. Surely they'd never use anything so dangerous. But whatever was in the oil was certainly having a strange effect. She'd never felt anything like the tingling, itchy pleasure that seemed to radiate around the whole of her lower belly. Steven moved close and she writhed a little, arching her back as his fingers began stroking the hard bud of her clit.

That tiny organ seemed to have swollen to ten times its size. She imagined it as a little red cock, thrusting hungrily towards the potent pleasures of Steven's oily touch. He took Marika's clitoris between finger and thumb, pinching it and moving it up and down.

Marika screwed her eyes shut, cried out, and orgasmed, feeling her vagina pulse and push out wantonly towards Steven as if begging for his attention. When the first waves of pleasure had faded, she opened her eyes and saw that the Major had positioned himself behind Lisa.

His thin cheeks were flushed and his eyes bright as he lifted Lisa's short skirt and pulled down her frilly white knickers. Lisa smiled at Marika, her eyes glazed with lust, as she leaned forward to accommodate the Major.

'Now the phallus, Steven,' the Major groaned,

his hands busy at work under Lisa's short skirt.

Steven unwrapped the scrap of red silk and drew out a carved ivory phallus.

'Scrimshaw. Made by whalers,' the Major said, hoarsely. 'Worth hundreds of pounds. Fine example.'

Steven held the object up, so that Marika could see that the phallus was beautifully carved and set into a base of ebony. His strong fingers caressed the ivory shaft, while his eyes held hers. His mouth was slack with desire and she thought that he would lean forward and kiss her in a moment, but he only said, 'Are you ready for this?'

Lisa groaned loudly as the Major threw her skirt over her back and mounted her. He grasped Lisa's buttocks, pulling them apart and began thrusting into her vagina. Steven anointed the phallus with more of the spicy oil and ran the head of it over Marika's splayed sex.

Marika couldn't help working her hips, pumping herself with total abandonment towards Steven's hand. Lisa's moans added an edge to her passion and she twisted, trying to rub her aching nub on the bulbous end of the phallus. Steven teased and stroked her, keeping her on the brink of an orgasm for what seemed like ages.

Marika could feel the syrupy juices trickling down her folds. The leather cloth was slippery under her. She felt the juices pooling, lubricating the crease of her bottom and tickling against her anus. Some of the spicy oil had trickled onto her anus as well and she felt it like a second vagina, another needy orifice. Steven seemed to realise the fact. Slipping a finger between Marika's buttocks he began circling the creased brown rose with one finger.

'Oh yes. Oh God. Yes,' Marika moaned, beside herself with a raging lust. She hardly knew what she was saying. 'Fuck me with that thing, Steven. Do it to me, like in the book. Oh God. Please. Stick it right in.'

The Major's face was flushed red and the veins stood out on his forehead as he pumped away energetically at Lisa's pert backside. Lisa chewed at her bottom lip, grunting and moaning, her body moving with the force of the Major's assault.

'That's it, darling. Oh, that's it,' the Major cried. 'Squeeze it. Take it. By God, what a woman!'

And Marika didn't know who he was speaking to, but it didn't matter. They were all four locked within their own bodies, prisoners of their senses, sharing the experience, but feeling the intensity of it in their different degrees.

Marika lifted her hips from the table and surged towards Steven's hands, wanting, needing to be penetrated. If she didn't get relief soon, she thought she might faint. The special ingredient in the oil had provoked a reaction she could hardly believe.

She felt like the embodiment of pure sexual energy – like the Indian love-goddess, Rati. When Steven leaned over her and slipped one finger into her anus and the phallus deeply into her vagina, she screamed and came again, but it still wasn't enough. Her sex was awash, weeping pearls of milky fluid, the cloth slippery with her oily outpourings.

The Major gave a great cry and collapsed onto Lisa's back. Lisa put her hands under her own skirt, made a few rapid movements and grunted as she orgasmed. She stood with her head bent, catching her breath.

Steven had let go of the phallus, leaving it sticking out of Marika's body. It began slowly to slip out of her, the ebony base knocking on the table. His hands went to the waistband of his trousers. In a moment his cock sprang free, rearing up potently, the shaft topped by a shiny, plum-like head.

Reaching out he removed the phallus, grasped Marika by the hips, and pulled her to the edge of the table. She felt the leather cloth slide under her and then her buttocks were hanging in mid air and Steven's hands were cradling the firm globes. He lifted her up and onto his glans, nudging her swollen flesh open before sheathing himself inside her.

As Steven began thrusting strongly into her, Marika tossed her head back and forth in a frenzy. Orgasms ripped through her, blending together so that she lost track of how many times she came.

The pleasure was finally too much. The room seemed to darken at the edges, she felt her hold on reality slipping away. The last ripples of sensation spread spidery fingers deep into her womb and she sank back amongst the cushions, senseless.

CHAPTER 11

When Marika came back to herself, it was to find Lisa sponging her face with a cool cloth which smelt of cologne.

'Wake up now, Marika,' she whispered. 'That's it. You gave me quite a fright for a moment. Your capacity for pleasure is astonishing. I shouldn't think Steven will forget his visit in a hurry!'

Marika pushed herself up against the cushions and looked down the table at the Major who was putting the leather-covered book back in the bookcase. Steven was dressed and sitting back in one of the red leather chairs. As she watched he stretched luxuriously and flashed her a grin.

The Major moved away from the bookcase. Beaming at Marika, he said, 'Feeling better now, my dear? You're a little pale. I expect your hungry after expending so much energy. I had Cook prepare a meal earlier. We'd all be delighted if you'd share it with us.'

Marika felt exhausted, but she was conscious of being very hungry too. 'Thank you. I'd love to stay and eat with you.'

She got down from the table and on the Major's suggestion went off with Lisa to the bathroom to freshen up.

'There's everything we need here,' Lisa said. 'Do you want the bath or the shower?'

Marika chose the bath and stripped off as she ran the water. She would have preferred to be alone, but Lisa's company was not intrusive. It ought to have seemed strange to be sharing a bathroom with another woman, but in the circumstances it would have been ridiculous to be shy. isa stepped out of the maid's outfit, revealing an enviably slim figure, and disappeared into the shower cubicle. Marika poured bath essence into the stream of water and lowered herself into the bath. The effects of the oil seemed to have mostly worn off and Marika was conscious only of a residual warmth and a slight tingling around her sex and inside her vagina. The feeling was not unpleasant.

Lisa finished her shower and stepped back into the room. She began towelling her hair dry. While Marika was soaking in a bath filled with creamy, rose-scented oil there was a knock at the door and an older woman poked her head into the room. She introduced herself as the housekeeper and held out a kimono of black silk, embroidered with a gold design.

'The Major thought you might like to wear this, madam. If you'd like to give your other clothes to me I'll see that they are laundered.'

'Thanks,' Marika smiled.

Lisa finished drying herself, ran her fingers through her hair, and donned her maid's uniform.

'I'll leave you to it,' she said. Bending over the

bath, she kissed Marika's cheek. Her short brown curls were fluffed around her head like a damp halo. 'That was some performance back there! A real turn-on. Maybe we'll meet you again sometime. Take care.'

'Aren't you staying for dinner?'

'No. I've things to do. Bye now.'

Marika was rather disappointed that Lisa wasn't staying. She had wanted to ask her what her connection with the Major was. She had noticed that the pendant Lisa wore bore a single heart – just like Pia's. Did that mean that they occupied the same place in the hierarchy?

After bathing, Marika used a number of the perfumed toiletries which lined the shelves of the bathroom. There were a large number of products, all of them lushly perfumed and decanted into antique cut-glass containers. She wondered how often the Major had house guests.

The dinner was superb. Salmon in dill sauce, steamed baby vegetables, and raspberry soufflé. The housekeeper served the food, paying no attention to the fact that Marika was eating her meal dressed only in the kimono.

Steven had changed into a black, crew-necked shirt and a biscuit-coloured suit. During the meal she learned that he was a business colleague of the Major's and was based in Holland. The Major was the perfect host and kept up a stream of animated conversation. After a while they all moved to the lounge for coffee and brandy.

'I expect that you've been wondering about my connection with the Discipline of Pearls?' the Major said to Marika.

She had in fact given the matter some thought as she bathed, although she hadn't expected the

Major to be so candid. There seemed no necessity for him to bring the matter up, but he obviously wanted to talk about it.

'My own great-grandfather was one of a group of individuals who started the society back in the eighteen-thirties,' the Major said proudly. 'The early Victorians weren't at all the prudes they were made out to be, you know. Great-grandfather was a true sensualist. He began the collection, part of which you've seen. By the way, the anniversary I spoke of earlier – it's the date when he began the collection. I'm merely a custodian. On my death it will pass on to someone suitable within the society.'

Marika smiled. 'It seems that I'm in very illustrious company. I've never met an elder of the society before.'

'One elder and one who is aspiring to be,' Steven said. 'You can see that we're just people like anyone else.'

Not like anyone else that she knew, Marika thought, accepting another measure of brandy. It was obvious that both men were very wealthy as well as charismatic. Steven had an air of strength and authority about him. She suspected that all the elders, both men and women, would have this quality.

She sipped her brandy with relish, listening as the Major spoke about his rare books and the various items in the collection of erotica. She found herself becoming more and more fascinated. She had always loved books and reading, and many of the items in the Major's collection had a long and curious history.

The Major seemed gratified by her genuine interest in his subject. Presently he stopped speaking and gave her a searching look. After satisfying himself on some score, he began speaking as if on impulse.

'Forgive my frankness, but I feel that I have to put a proposition to you. How would you like to work for me?'

She hid her surprise. 'I don't have the time, I'm afraid. I have a demanding job already.'

'This wouldn't interfere with your regular work. It's society business. You could dictate your own hours. I'd pay you very well.'

She started to protest, but he held up his hand.

'Let me explain before you decide. I've been looking for someone to pass my expertise onto, someone who would be able to travel if necessary. Occasionally an important work of erotica comes onto the market. In the past I would pursue such a work and arrange any transaction personally, but I'm no longer a young man. I hardly leave the house these days.' He paused for effect. 'Would you consider acting as my agent?'

'You mean tracking down books like the ones in your collection and making an offer for them? I don't think I'd feel qualified.'

He made an airy gesture. 'But you would be if you were to come here and spend time amongst the books. I have catalogues, reference books, lists of the most important collections around the world. All of it's on disk. You could study the information in your spare time. There'd be no pressure. Just say you'll think about it. You'd be perfect. You're intelligent, used to making deals and handling people. And most of all you're destined for great things within the society. Don't think I haven't noticed the carving on your pendant.'

She saw his eyes stray to the pendant, which was visible inside the loose neckline of the kimono. For a moment longer, she hesitated, but she already knew that she'd agree. She liked the Major and it would be a joy to study the collection. Besides, as he said, she was well qualified for the position he offered.

'All right. I'll work for you,' she said.

He smiled broadly. 'Do you hear that, Steven? Excellent. I can't tell you how happy that makes me. I'll pay all your expenses of course and a fee for your services. And a retainer of . . . Let me see . . .'

He named an amount that made her swallow hard.

'That's far too much . . .'

He waved away her protests. 'Nonsense, you're worth every penny. Besides what else have I got to spend my money on? Now, this calls for a celebration. Let's crack open that new bottle of Armagnac. If you wouldn't mind doing the honours, Steven? It's on the tray on the bureau.'

'Oh please don't on my account,' Marika laughed. 'I really mustn't drink anymore. This has been a fascinating experience in every respect, but it's late. I think I ought to be going.'

Marika made a move to get up and her head swam alarmingly. She sat down again abruptly.

'I think you're already a few over the limit,' the Major said. 'I could call you a taxi . . . On second thought, why not stay the night? We have plenty of room, then you can start out in the morning with a clear head.'

Marika was tempted. After the food and wine, then brandy, she really didn't feel much like moving. Added to which the intensity of the sexual experience and the resulting sense of well-being had made her feel very languid.

'My car. It's parked outside the house . . .' she began in a half-hearted attempt at a protest.

'Don't worry, I'll bring it around the back,' Steven said equably. 'I'd stay if I were you. My friend here can be very determined.'

Both of them were treating her with such warmth and courtesy that she felt cocooned by a sense of security.

'I'm bushed actually. It'll be a relief not to have to drive back tonight.'

In the hall Steven took her hand and drew her towards him. His mouth brushed her cheek. 'It's been a pleasure,' he said. 'Sleep well.'

The housekeeper led her upstairs and showed her into a room which overlooked the garden. She turned on a bedside lamp and the small room was flooded with a wash of green and gold, reflected from the stained glass of a Tiffany lampshade.

Marika was so tired that she slipped off the kimono and got straight into the bed. Pulling the quilted comforter up to her chin, she fell asleep immediately.

The sound of birdsong woke her. For a moment she couldn't remember where she was. She glanced at her watch and saw that it was six a.m.

Padding across the room, she drew the heavy velvet curtains and let the sunlight into the room. She could see the garden below, a well tended expanse of greenery and pale blooms – white, pale-blue, peach – more suited to the British light than the garish colours many people planted. It all looked as perfect as a photograph from a gardening magazine. Beyond the shrubbery at the back, she could see the gleaming blue paintwork of her car.

Turning back into the room, she went to reach for her kimono. There was a knock at the door and the housekeeper appeared with her clothes, freshly laundered and pressed.

'The Major hopes that you'll join him for breakfast before you leave.'

'I've only time for a coffee. I have to get back to my flat and change before I start out for the office. Is Steven joining us?'

'He had an early flight to catch. He left the house at five a.m. Is there anything else I can do for you, madam?'

'No, thank you. I'll be down shortly.'

Marika began to dress as soon as the woman left. So the peck on the cheek last night had been Steven's way of saying goodbye. She didn't expect that they'd meet again and she was happy to have it that way.

In the light of day, Marika was embarrassed at the way the voile dress revealed the lines of her body. Her breasts were barely concealed by the thin fabric, but there was nothing to be done about that.

She was about to leave the bedroom when something caught her eye. A photograph, framed in silver, stood on a dresser. She hadn't noticed it before, as it stood in the shadow of the curtain.

Her heart missed a beat. Staring back at her, some years younger, but plainly recognisable, was the face of Stone.

Marika picked up the photograph. Stone's hair was longer and swept back from his forehead. She saw the resemblance to the Major at once. Was Stone the Major's son? It was possible. The family connection with the secret society was strong.

In the photograph Stone wore a black turtle neck sweater and slim, dark trousers. He was leaning against the door of a summerhouse, a black labrador at his feet. The photograph had been taken in the Major's garden – she had seen the summerhouse from the bedroom window.

She'd ask the Major about Stone at the first opportunity.

Marika drank her breakfast coffee in the dining room. She was half-way through a cup, before the Major put in an appearance.

'Ah, I'm glad you haven't left. Sorry to hold you up. I'm a late riser these days. My health isn't so good. But the fact that you're going to be working for me is the best tonic I can think of.'

Marika smiled, sipping the aromatic coffee. 'I'm going to enjoy it. I'm doing it for me too,' She paused. 'I . . . couldn't help noticing the photograph in the room upstairs. Is that young man a relative?'

'A real heart-breaker, isn't he?' the Major smiled. 'That's Jordan, my nephew. He's the closest thing I have to a son. My late wife and I never had children.'

Marika tried not to appear too inquisitive, but inside she was quivering with tension.

'What does St . . . I mean Jordan do?'

'He works in the City, in computers. Very top notch. He's a young man who's going places. I don't see him as often as I'd like to these days. I virtually brought Jordan up when his mother died. He never got over her death, you see. And his own father was too busy with his own grief to notice how much his son was hurting.'

The Major's eyes misted over when he spoke about the boy he remembered. Marika laid a hand on his arm. The old man blinked and smiled sadly. In the morning light he looked less vital and his skin had a yellowish tinge. He gave Marika a searching look. She wasn't quick enough to hide her expression.

'You've already met him. Through the society,' he said. It was a statement, rather than a question.

'Yes,' Marika said softly.

The Major's lips thinned. 'I should have realised that sooner. You're a beautiful, intelligent and accomplished young woman. Just the type we like to recruit to our number. I shouldn't think Jordan could resist you. Did he present you with the pendant personally? It would be just like him to bend the rules.'

Marika smiled, impressed by the Major's powers of deduction. She nodded.

'He came up to me in the car park below my office and told me that the pendant was something I'd come to value. And I have. I can hardly remember a time before the Discipline of Pearls. I'd . . . I'd like to see Jordan again though. He's elusive to say the least.'

The Major poured himself some fresh coffee.

'Looks like Jordan made quite an impression on you. If you take my advice, you won't become too attached to him. I'm very fond of him, but I'm not blind to his faults. Jordan's a cold man. There's a bond between many of us above a certain level in the society, but my nephew prefers to remain aloof. I had hoped that we would remain close and that in time . . . Well, Jordan goes his own way.'

'I've realised that,' Marika said ruefully. 'In

some strange way Jordan and I are involved. I can't explain how. That's just the way it is, although I know that he's fighting admitting it. I know we'll meet face to face eventually.'

The Major looked doubtful. 'Jordan is a law unto himself. He despises weakness, in himself and others. If you want to be happy, don't fall under his spell.'

It was probably good advice, Marika thought, but it had come way too late. She was as closely involved with Stone as it was possible to be – without being a Siamese twin. Finishing her coffee, she shook the Major's hand before she left. Then on impulse embraced him. He pressed a gift-wrapped package into Marika's hands.

'I want you to have this,' he said. 'Goodbye for now. I'll be in touch about that business we discussed.'

Although she smiled at the Major, Marika felt vaguely depressed. The more she found out about Stone, the less she knew him. Why did he have to be so elusive? Sometimes I wish I'd never met you, Jordan Stone, she thought.

Back at the flat Marika opened the little parcel.

Inside was a beautifully bound booklet. She turned the pages to find that it was an erotic poem, illustrated in the style of Beardsley. Tucked inside was a black card with a gold embossed phone number.

She smiled to herself as she placed the booklet on her dressing table. The Major was a perfect gentleman. He'd even managed to make the act of passing her the card for her next assignment into a charming gesture. She understood also, that their working arrangement was to be viewed as something quite separate from the normal workings of the society.

Slipping out of the white voile dress, she changed into a plain chocolate-brown suit, worn over a cream blouse with guipure lace revers. Brushing her hair forward, she swept it up into a knot on top of her head and secured it with two ivory-coloured combs.

She smiled at herself in the mirror as she clipped on a pair of chunky amber earrings. She looked the perfect woman-about-town, sophisticated and groomed to within an inch of her life.

No one would ever guess that she'd spent the previous night lying on her back with her dress rucked up and her legs spread wide open, enjoying the most exquisite sexual pleasure at the hands of complete strangers.

She'd come so many times that she'd actually passed out. How extraordinary that she hadn't known that there were such heights to reach. For years she'd been only mildly interested in sex. She had the same body, the same mind, but her responses lately seemed to be zooming right off the Richter scale. She wondered what else there was to experience. Surely a person could only take so much pleasure.

She felt a tingle of wantonness, deep inside her. It would certainly be fun finding out if that was true.

She looked forward to working for the Major. Learning all about rare works of erotica and travelling the world in search of more books would be an exciting and challenging experience. She was sure to meet others from within the society, powerful and attractive men. The prospect was a pleasing one.

Powdering her nose and applying fresh lipstick, she left for the office.

While driving to work, Marika's thoughts revolved around Stone. It seemed that he was a mystery to those who knew him best. She pictured the lonely, grieving little boy whom the Major had taken care of.

No wonder he was remote and unwilling to form attachments with others – especially women. The Discipline of Pearls provided him with a cloak of anonymity. Inside the society he could indulge himself in every way possible, while withdrawing to a safe emotional distance.

Marika felt more determined than ever to meet him face to face. It seemed to her that something about his character appealed to the perversity in her own nature. We've put our mark on each other, Stone, she thought, whether or not you want to face up to that fact.

And I intend to make you acknowledge me.

The next few days were as hectic as ever. Marika had no time to think to think of anything but work.

By mid-week she knew that she needed a break. Another postcard from Pia had arrived in the post and Marika experienced pangs of loneliness as she read it. She could have phoned the number on the card the Major had given her, but somehow the thought of a sexual encounter with a total stranger was not appealing. She needed contact with a friend.

Phoning Gwen, she told her that she wouldn't be coming into the office that day. Gwen's surprise was palpable. Marika couldn't remember the last time she'd played truant.

'What is it? A cold? Hangover?' Gwen said.

Marika grinned. 'I think the French call it *le malaise*. Translated that means "I'm in dire need of a day off". Will you fend off anything urgent for me? I'll be in tomorrow for definite.'

'Okay,' Gwen said. 'Whatever you do today, make it count. And have one for me.'

Marika smiled. Gwen was too clever for her own good. Dialling again, she waited for Rafael to answer his phone.

'Hello?'

'Rafael. It's Marika. Can you take some time off today? I've a yen for seeing the countryside from the back of a Harley.'

'You got it. Come on over. I'm all yours. I've got a spare set of leathers and a helmet. We can leave as soon as you get here.'

His enthusiasm was infectious. She liked his willingness to drop everything and fall in with her plans. The thought of his beautiful face and strong young body made her body tighten with need. Rafael was strong, warm, and appreciative. And he was good company. Just what she needed today.

He was waiting outside the huge wooden doors as she drove up in the BMW. On one gate there was a hastily scribbled sign which read 'Closed All Day'.

Rafael was already zipped into his motorbike leathers, his limbs encased in the shiny black fabric and padded at elbow and knee. He closed the garage doors when she'd parked her car. Holding out the spare suit, he said,

'You can change here. I'm not expecting anyone.'

'Okay.'

Holding eye contact with him, she slipped off

her outer clothes, letting her navy skirt and blouse slip to the floor. His lips pursed in a long whistle of appreciation as her scantily clad body came into view.

She wore a half-cup bra and G-string in French navy see-through net. Matching lace-top hold-up stockings and navy courts were her only other garments.

'You've got no business looking that good,' Rafael grinned, reaching for her and burying his face in her neck.

She laughed and threaded her fingers in his hair. The shiny strands were freshly washed. His cheeks were smooth and cool and his mouth was firm on hers. He tasted of peppermint. As he pulled her close, she could feel his erection pressing into her thigh.

'We're not in too much of a hurry to be off, are we?' she said huskily, leading him over to the line of custom built Harleys.

He watched her, his chest rising and falling rapidly under the casing of black leather, as she straddled the nearest motorbike and leaned back along the big padded seat. The bike was beautiful, a gleaming chrome beast, upholstered in wine-coloured leather.

Running her hands up her body Marika cupped her breasts, kneading their fullness and lifting them so that they bulged provocatively upwards. She enjoyed having the power to arouse him. It was an extra turn-on to have a young man so hot for her.

'What are you waiting for?' she said teasingly.

The sound of a zip opening was loud in the silence. Rafael dug his thumbs into his waistband, slipping down his leather trousers and his black briefs in a single movement. His cock jutted forward, hard and ready. Marika writhed on the seat, lifting her hips towards him, thrusting the bulge of her pubis wantonly at him. She knew that the flattened curls of her pubes and the moist opening of her sex was visible through the fine net.

'Good God,' Rafael, breathed straddling the seat and reaching out to encircle her waist. 'Come here, woman.'

His stiff shaft reared up between them, throbbing and already moist with a tiny drop of pre-come. She could smell the salty tang of male arousal. Smoothing on a condom hurriedly, he pulled Marika towards him, fitting her spread legs over his muscular thighs.

His fingers caressed the pouting shape of her through the net, and she rubbed herself against him like a cat being petted. She felt Rafael's hand at her waist; a sharp tug and he'd torn the G-string free of her sex.

The underwear set had cost a fortune, but she didn't care that it was ruined. It had served its purpose. She threw back her head and murmured with delight as Rafael lifted her, spread her buttocks with his hands and slid her onto the bulbous head of his cock. He lowered her slowly, feeding himself into her by degrees, all the time watching her face.

'Oh, go slowly. Slowly.'

She bit her lip as her tight vagina opened to him. She wasn't really wet yet and his cock felt very big as it sought to enter her. But it felt so damned good that she couldn't wait to be filled by him.

Then Rafael jammed her down hard on the

final inch. She grunted as he slid his full length into her, the head wedging tight against her womb.

'Oh you bastard,' she breathed, squirming against him, rubbing her swollen teats against his chest, the fine mesh of the bra slipping aside to cut across her nipples.

The red-brown cones peeped rudely out of the bra and Rafael bent his head to graze at them with his lips. Holding her tightly around the waist, he lifted her up and down, working her on the rigid cudgel of his flesh. Marika's buttocks churned against his spread thighs as little spears of sensation flowed down from her nipples and centred in the warm cavern of her woman-flesh.

Now she was wet, the slippery juices flowing around him. Bouncing up and down in time with his thrusts she gasped and moaned with the pleasure of being so soundly plundered. She buried her face in the hollow of Rafael's shoulder and bit her lip as she climaxed. His strong arms around her made her feel safe and wanted. Just as she needed to feel.

Later, with the wind tearing at her body as she clung to Rafael, the Harley's engine purring under her, she felt light-hearted and carefree. Rafael's muscles moved under the leather jacket as he leaned the motorbike into a tight bend.

Marika lifted her face and felt the sun pouring down on her. The light through the trees, spattered them with strobes of silver and black.

A sense of contentment settled over her.

She'd almost managed to do what she'd set out to - put aside her obsession with Stone.

CHAPTER

12

The sleek, chauffeur-driven Mercedes left Pisa airport and headed inland.

Marika leant back against the tan leather seats and closed her eyes. She had dozed a little during the night flight, but not enough for her to feel rested. Now she had the light-headed feeling that came from lack of sleep coupled with mental alertness.

She had telephoned the number on the card the night after she returned from meeting Rafael. The voice on the telephone had been a woman's, cool and impersonal. 'Your flight is booked. A car will meet you at Galileo Galilei. Expect to stay in Tuscany for the weekend.'

There had been no other conversation. Marika had simply agreed to take the assignment. The only difference, this time, was that she was travelling in the early morning.

The chauffeur handled the beautiful car with practised expertise, exhibiting none of the schizoid temperament of many Italian drivers. The roads were deserted at this hour, the sun just touching the hills of Tuscany with a rosy dawn light. The car's air conditioning was a cool caress against her stockinged legs.

She had freshened her make-up at the airport and smoothed the creases out of her fine wool jacket and slim skirt, but she longed for a shower and a change of clothes.

As the sun came up, the green rolling hills and fertile plains became visible through the mist. Gentle slopes covered with vines and olive groves were illuminated by a deep yellow glow. Umbrella pines and cypresses fringed the dusty road.

Marika watched the grey-tiled farmhouses slide past and wondered when they would reach their destination. She asked the chauffeur where they were going, but he only grunted and pointed ahead. She hadn't really expected him to tell her. They drove for about an hour before the towers of a fortressed hill-town came into view.

'San Gimignano,' the chauffeur said, pointing in the direction of the dozen or so towers of pinkish-grey stone.

The splendid city walls rose up before them as the Mercedes purred towards the south gate. Cruising down the main street of the town, they climbed the short rise which led to a piazza surrounded by tall buildings of the same pink and grey weathered stone.

Marika looked out at the narrow streets, shaded by towers and houses with green slatted shutters. Emerging into a small square, where the houses had wrought-iron balconies and flowering creepers adorning their walls, the car drew to a halt. Marika opened the tinted car window a fraction and the smells from a nearby bakery drifted towards her.

Her stomach cramped. But she wasn't hungry. She had the now familiar feeling of fear of the unknown, coupled with mounting sexual excitement. She imagined that lustful dark eyes were watching her from behind the shutters.

She uncrossed her legs, the satin lining of her skirt flowing against her skin, and waited for the chauffeur to open the door for her, but he made no move to get out. Puzzled, she leaned forward to tap him on the shoulder, then hesitated when a movement caught her eye. The door to a nearby house opened and a man and woman came out and walked towards the car.

Marika recognised them at once. Stone was lightly tanned, immaculate in a pale blue linen suit, Raybans shading his eyes. Pia wore a simple shift of black silk-jersey. Her dark hair was slicked straight back into a glossy cap. She wore huge, ethnic-style earrings set with red stones.

Stone's arm was curved possessively around Pia's waist. She leaned into him, laughing up into his shaded eyes. It was plain that they'd just spent the night together. Marika felt a flicker of jealousy, but she didn't know which of them had prompted it.

It was a shock to find them together, but she determined not to show Stone that she was disconcerted. He knew about the closeness she shared with Pia. What game was he playing now?

As the couple drew nearer, the chauffeur got out and opened the rear door of the car. The tinted windows hid Marika from view until Pia bent down to get into the back seat.

'Darling!' she said flinging herself into the car and embracing Marika. 'What a wonderful surprise. How did you find us?'

Marika smiled coolly at Stone who was removing his sunglasses. 'Ask him. He arranged for this assignation. Didn't you?'

Pia glanced at Stone. 'Why didn't you tell me that Marika was coming here?'

He seated himself next to Pia. 'I wanted to surprise you both. I hope you're well, Marika. I've been hearing good things about you. So you're to work for the Major? You're rising fast within the society.'

'Still prying into my affairs?' she said tartly. 'Do you know everything I've been doing and with whom?'

He flashed her his narrow grin, showing his perfect white teeth. Marika felt as if she'd been slammed hard in the solar plexis. She had remembered his looks – high-cheekbones, deep-set eyes and that sculptured mouth – but she had forgotten his absolute self-possession, the simmering power of his persona.

'But of course. I know everything about everyone in the society,' Stone said. 'It's my life. And you've surprised me, Marika. Not many people manage to do that. You make a strong impression on everyone you meet. The Major speaks highly of you. Rafael, is enamoured of you. Pia here has been singing your praises – although not all night, I'm glad to say.'

Stone picked up Pia's hand and brought it to his lips. Pia's little pink tongue snaked out to lick his fingers. Marika had a mental image of them making love; Stone's finely muscled body covering Pia; Pia kneeling between his thighs, her mouth stretched around his erect cock; Stone flipping Pia onto her belly and driving into her, ramming himself between her raised buttocks.

The pictures were potent and starkly erotic. Marika blushed as Stone pinned her with his steely gaze. He knew exactly what she was thinking. She was the first to look away. The insistent flutter between her thighs was disturbing. How was it that she responded to him in a purely physical way, even when she was angry with him for manipulating her?

He knew that she had wanted to meet him alone. And he was well aware of the chemistry between them. Why bring Pia along?

Pia gave a soft laugh as she looked from one to the other.

'Oh you two! Just look at you. Bristling like fighting cats.' She leaned towards Marika, her mouth brushing her cheek. 'I've missed you,' she whispered, her lips moving towards Marika's mouth.

Marika turned into her kiss, her mouth opening under the crushed-flower sweetness of Pia's lips. She put her arms around her and pulled her close, feeling Pia's slender limbs and her firm breasts pressing against her own.

'I've missed you too,' she murmured.

'How touching,' Stone said dryly.

Marika smiled at him, her lips curving wickedly. He sounded displeased. Perhaps she was supposed to be furious with him for sleeping with Pia. Was that what he expected? She felt that she'd scored a point, but she knew that Stone wouldn't allow her to feel any triumph.

He was the sort of man who planned things carefully. What *was* he up to? Then, in a flash, she knew. This whole set-up was for her benefit. To bring her into line. She had been behaving too independently, making up her own rules as she went along.

And Stone didn't like that. She was *his* protégée. Her actions reflected on him. Stone was showing her that he had an equal hold over both her and Pia. He was testing her to see how far she'd go. Would she still want him?

Damn him, she thought inwardly. He was half right about her. She was hungry for him, ravenous, and the bastard knew it. Pia's presence made no difference.

Stone placed Pia's hand on Marika's thigh.

'Why don't you become reacquainted, in full?' he said coolly. 'It's been a while since I sampled Marika's beautiful body. I intend to do so again. And as soon as possible. Get her wet for me, Pia.'

Pia's lovely face lit up with desire. Marika knew that she'd do as Stone ordered. Her eyes widenened in shock. The bastard. He meant to have her right here, while the car sped along the country roads, and the chauffeur watched them in the driving mirror.

Stone's eyes held a challenge. Are you brave enough for this? they seemed to say. Marika was tempted to tell him to go straight to hell, but she knew that she wouldn't. She had wanted to prompt a reaction from him. And she had. It was far too late to complain that she had had something else in mind. Something private, more intimate.

The unexpected was Stone's forte. She had known that all along. That had been part of the challenge.

Keeping Pia's hand covered with his own, Stone pushed Marika's skirt up slowly, so slowly, until her smooth thighs and stocking tops were revealed. Stone made the gesture, but it was Pia's touch she felt.

'Lovely,' he breathed. 'Such creamy skin.'

His hands pushed her skirt up higher, the satin lining slipping against her bottom as it was rucked up into creases around her waist. Her suspender belt was a wisp of cream satin and her matching French knickers were flared and lace-trimmed. The loose legs had become twisted and the crotch was pulled tightly to one side of her mound where the light brown hair of her pubis was visible.

She half-closed her eyes as Pia's hand slipped into her crotch and began stroking her exposed mound.

Stone's dark eyes studied her face intently, watching the play of emotion across her face. Wriggling on the seat, Marika attempted to push her skirt down and close her legs, but she was acutely aware of the sudden rush of heat to her lower belly. Her sex bulged to one side of the gusset and her wetness was gathering behind the tight-pressed lips.

'Please . . . no. I can't . . .'

Stone laughed. 'What's wrong, Marika? Not shy, are you? Not after raising your hips to me in the hotel room and grinding down onto my prick? Not after spreading your legs on that stage in Paris and letting everyone see how wet and swollen you were? You let Steven massage oil into your sex and fuck you with the ivory phallus until you passed out with pleasure. Surely you're not refusing to take part in this assignment? Remember the society's rules. You made the phone call.'

Marika gasped. Stone's words were scandalous, crude, and horribly exciting. How could he know all those intimate details? Pia's eyes were gleaming with mounting excitement as she stroked Marika's pubic floss, working gradually inwards to her pulsing centre. Her fingers were ticklish against the soft curls, pressing them away from the closed slit.

When Stone leaned over and kissed her, Marika moaned against his mouth. Her hips left the leather seat in an involuntary little thrusting movement as his tongue pushed strongly into her mouth. Oh God, she had forgotten how he tasted; musky-sweet, fresh, and so sexual.

Marika felt her will to resist slipping away. She wanted him badly. It was all true. She had done the things he'd listed, in private and public, and experienced the most incredible orgasms. But she'd never been spread in this way, ordered to perform in the glare of daylight, under the direct and intimately searching gaze of *this* man. The one man whom she desired above all others.

She shouldn't be excited by the way he was treating her, but she couldn't help it. It was his closeness, his intense dark gaze, the way he forced her to face up to her deepest and darkest desires – all of those things fanned both her shame and her passions.

Drawing away, Stone looked down at her, one slim finger pressing against her mouth.

'Feel her, Pia. Is she wet enough for me yet?'

Marika's eyelids fluttered as Pia's gentle fingers parted the thickening flesh-lips. She slid one finger into the moist groove and caressed Marika's intimate folds.

'Relax and enjoy it, my love. Remember Paris,' Pia whispered as her fingertip pressed on the swollen bud of Marika's clit and then began to move around it in tiny circles.

Marika's legs scissored wildly. She couldn't bear to be so aroused, so horribly vulnerable. But she couldn't help it. The bright daylight, the three other people who were watching her, added an extra dimension to her excitement. Her sex pulsed and tingled and her vagina was wet and needy.

'No. Oh no . . .' she moaned.

'That's it. Struggle a little with yourself. I love your fire and the way you fight yourself.' Stone's voice was deep, hypnotic. 'Sumptuous, isn't she, Pia?'

'Mmmm,' Pia said, intent on pressing back the lips of Marika's sex, so that her deep-pink folds and strongly erect clit were revealed to Stone's gaze.

Marika moaned as his hands slipped inside her jacket and caressed her breasts which were pressing against her stretch-cotton top. He dipped one hand into the low neck and grasped each breast, dragging it free almost roughly. Oh God, she couldn't stand it. She knew how she must look with her skirt pulled up, her jacket gaping open. The full mounds of her breasts were jutting obscenely over the dragged-down neck of her top, each nipple a prominent and aching stub.

Her eyes flew to the driving mirror and met the calm gaze of the chauffeur. Suddenly it was too much. With the shame burning in her cheeks, Stone's intense dark eyes on her face, she surged against Pia's hand and came. With her own breathy cries echoing in her ears, Marika squeezed her eyes shut.

'She's ready now,' Stone said huskily. 'Move aside, Pia.'

While the internal flutters were still gripping Marika's womb, Stone moved in close and flipped her over. She groaned in protest as she felt the leather seat under her belly, her cheek pressed into the seat-back. In the cramped space she was in a kneeling position, her legs trailing on the car floor.

Marika sobbed with shame as Stone's hands dragged at her French knickers. He left them lodged around her knees and used his leg to nudge her thighs apart. Even while she writhed away from him, hating the way he handled her with such ease of ownership, she found herself arching her back and lifting her soaking sex towards him.

Stone grasped her around the waist, his hands digging into her and pulling her against him. There was a moment while he pulled on a condom, then she felt his cock probing at her sex. It was hot and hard and she whimpered when he pushed into her entrance, paused, then went into her in one long fluid movement. She felt his muscled thighs slamming against hers as he began plundering her innermost depths.

Marika's mouth was crushed against the leather seat-back. She grunted with each inward thrust. Stone drew partway out of her, rimming her entrance with his big covered glans. Then he slid out of her and she almost cried out with disappointment.

Sliding a hand under her, Stone ran his fingers up along her parted folds and pinched her clit. The twin-edged prickle of pain and pleasure made her gasp and she writhed on the seat. Her bare breasts rubbed against the leather and she longed for a rougher, more hurting touch.

As if she could read her mind, Pia slipped her hands under Marika and began stroking and squeezing her nipples. Pia murmured endearments, her soft mouth moving over Marika's cheeks and mouth. Marika's sex pulsed and throbbed as Pia's and Stone's fingers worked at her, but she longed for his cock to possess her again. Why did he deny her that?

Then she felt a new and shocking sensation. And with mounting horror, she understood.

His fingers were edging her buttocks apart, smoothing some kind of lubricant up the damp crease. Two fingers were working the oily substance into her anus, probing inside her rectum. She felt herself bearing down, rebelling against this final imposition. Not that. Oh no.

'Please, Stone. No . . . I don't want . . .'

'Oh yes, Marika. This is what *I* want,' Stone said, his voice hardly recognisable. 'And you'll love it. Just relax. Forget all the taboos and listen to what your body tells you.'

His cock pressed against her untried opening and the covered glans slid a little way into her. Marika tensed and cried out as the tight ring of muscle gave way to him. It hurt, but there was a hot, stinging pleasure in the centre of the discomfort.

Stone waited, holding himself just inside the closure of the tight orifice. He rubbed gently on her clit, bringing her back to the brink of another orgasm before he slid fully into her anus. The path his cock forged opened to him slowly and smoothly.

Marika groaned, tremors flickered over her belly as her womb contracted with dark and forbidden pleasures. She imagined the plug of flesh in her body, stretching high into her virgin pathway. His fingers filled her too, moving in and out of her slick vaginal passage, only a thin flesh-wall away from his shaft. Her clit seemed pushed out by the obstructions within her. It was a hard, aching little bead.

The sensations, layer upon layer, were appalling, exquisite. Far removed from anything she could have imagined.

And Stone was right. She loved it. Revelled in the erotic intensity of everything that was being done to her. She felt pleasure on a different level, and knew herself to be a mere mindless jumble of nerve endings.

This was the true meaning of sex object. But she didn't care. Just for now, she was a willing recipient, a mass of quivering female flesh, ripe for pleasuring by the invasive male.

The realisation flooded her with shame. It was so contrary to what she thought normally. Tears of humiliation squeezed from the corners of her eyes as Stone slid his fingers into her up to the knuckles, pressing gently on the sensitive pad of flesh behind her clitoris.

Marika panted, hardly daring to move. The sensation of being filled was so all-encompassing. She felt stretched to capacity, impaled, the sensation too strange, too alien for words. Stone moved inside her, gently at first, letting her get used to the idea of having his cock inside that forbidden place.

Marika wept and arched her back, eager now for whatever he wanted. Her body had capitulated, but her mind still rebelled. She couldn't allow any man to treat her like this. It was wrong to want these things. To revel in being held down, oiled and violated. But Stone had known that she'd love being used in this way.

'God. Oh God. No, I can't . . .' she wept, her mouth lolling open, mashing against the leather seat-covering.

Pia cupped her breasts, massaging and rolling her aching nipples; her soft mouth nudged Marika's hair aside and nibbled at the sensitive nape of her neck.

'Shhh,' Pia murmured. 'It's all right to enjoy it. Give in to it. That's it. Reach for the pleasure. It isn't wrong.'

Knowing that Pia understood, had experienced the same awakening, loosened something in Marika. She bucked and cried out as she climaxed, her vagina convulsing around Stone's fingers as he pounded her bottom, boring into her.

The pleasure wrenched through her, centring on her entire lower belly. Stone gave a hoarse cry of release and buried himself into the very core of her, his thighs trembling against hers as he emptied himself.

Marika felt him collapse onto her, bearing part of his weight on his outspread hands. She saw the ring on his little finger and experienced a sense of déjà vu – only this time she was not blindfolded and buckled into a leather bodysuit.

Pia stroked her damp hair back from her forehead while Stone withdrew and wiped her clean. She smelt the lemony tang of some sort of cleansing tissues as Stone attended to them both. She still lay face down, hunched up on the seat, not caring that the chauffeur was probably looking at her bottom and spread legs.

Her face burned as Stone wiped her own pearly moisture from her inner thighs. She knew that her make-up was smudged and her cheeks were tear-stained. Stone didn't say a word, but he bent forward and she felt his warm lips pressing against first one buttock and then the other.

'Delightful sweet Marika,' Stone breathed. 'It's the way you rebel against your instincts for pleasure that makes you so enticing. Your final submission is all the more enjoyable.'

Marika didn't trust herself to speak. Reaching out, she found Pia's hand and clasped it tight. She didn't think she could bear to look Stone in the eye ever again.

Yet she knew that she would have to. He wasn't the sort of man who would leave things as they were. She knew that he wanted more of her, as she wanted more of him. But he wouldn't always have the upper hand.

They had been speeding along the curving roads of Tuscany and she realised that they had reached another town. The Mercedes slowed down and swept to a halt in front of a converted farmhouse.

Suddenly afraid that the chauffeur would open the door and find her with her skirt still rucked up, her knickers around her knees and her breasts exposed, Marika turned around and adjusted her clothes. Sitting with her knees pressed modestly together, she stared forward at the back of the chauffeur's neck.

From the tail of her eye, she saw that Stone was seated beside Pia, gazing serenely out of the window, a smile of satisfaction on his lean, handsome face. Pia smiled at Marika and patted her hand.

'You were wonderful,' she whispered. 'Watching you and Stone made me so hot.'

As the chauffeur got out and opened the car

door, Stone turned towards them both and said equably, 'Welcome to my house. I've had rooms prepared for you. You might like to bathe and change, then join me for drinks on the terrace.'

Marika forced herself to get out of the car slowly and walk towards the farmhouse. The chauffeur's face was impassive. She wondered how many other such incidents he'd witnessed.

Inside the farmhouse it was cool and spacious. The white walls were hung with paintings. The grey stone floor was covered with rugs and there were a number of antique cabinets and small tables. Two enormous sofas upholstered in white leather dominated the room.

Pia and Marika were shown to two rooms on the upper floor. As soon as they were alone, Pia came to Marika's room. She embraced Marika. They kissed affectionately. Pia rubbed herself against Marika, her hands cupping Marika's breasts.

'I'd like to make love to you now, at once,' Pia said, 'but I expect you're tired from the flight. And from . . . just now. Incredible, isn't he?' She reached up to touch Marika's cheek. 'I'm so horny from watching. Would you like to share a bath?'

Marika smiled. Pia was so tempting with her tilted dark eyes and her soft red mouth. The shape of her breasts were outlined by her plain black dress.

'You're a glutton for pleasure. Do you know that? But I'd like to be alone for a while. Do you mind?'

Pia grimaced, her mouth turning down at the corners with mock disappointment. 'Of course not. I'll keep. I'll see you later.'

Marika stripped off her clothes in the modern

en suite bathroom. She ran a bath and tipped perfumed oil under the stream of hot water. She needed to be alone to get her thoughts into order.

Easing herself into the sweetly scented water, she ran her hands over her body, conscious that she was washing away his smell and the last traces of the oil he'd used to gain access to her body.

She had been working up to this meeting, planning what she'd say to Stone when they met. Now Stone had managed to throw everything on its head. She had to face up to the fact that her emotions regarding him were more complicated than she'd realised.

By arranging this assignment – the ménage à trois in the back of the car – Stone was trying to show her that there was no room for individual relationships within the society. All kinds of sexual relationships were permissible, but God forbid that he should become emotionally attached to anyone. He'd asked her once, in his letter, why the thrill of the chase and the sex wasn't enough for her.

She grinned. Oh, you don't fool me, she thought. It's not enough for you either, but you can't handle that. He was trying to shape her into the only kind of woman he could cope with. A woman who cried and begged for him to pleasure her. Someone he could dominate, someone subordinate to his will.

And it was true that she *had* writhed under him, begged to be pleasured and loved every degrading moment of what he'd done to her. She wasn't ashamed of the fact now that she was calmer and able to think. To enjoy that kind of sex was just one facet of her erotic persona. She *did* want Stone in that particular way – the gut level, primaeval, take-me-I'm-yours, dominating male way.

What she had to make Stone understand was that she wasn't going to allow him to dominate her on any other level beyond the sexual. She was still the intelligent, independent, careerwoman, and she didn't need any man telling her what to do.

Whatever there was between her and Stone in the future would have to be on her terms.

Marika walked under the archway which led out to the terrace. Stone was waiting. He was seated at a table, a tray of drinks in front of him. He was freshly shaved and wearing an expensive, light-coloured suit.

On the table, next to the tray, there was a slim, black velvet box. He looked up and smiled at her, his deep-set eyes taking in her white linen dress and discreet jewellery.

He really was the most arresting man she'd ever seen. Her body sent out little tingles of remembered lust. It would be so easy to fall under his spell, to become a slave to the pleasure he gave her. But she knew that it would be a grave mistake to give in to him.

'Won't you sit down?' he said. 'Have a drink. The local Chianti is very good.'

'Thank you. I prefer to stand,' she said evenly.

His black eyebrows rose a fraction. 'As you wish.' He picked up the box and held it out to her. 'I have something for you. Open it.'

Marika lifted the lid and saw the pendant lying on the crumpled red satin. She picked up the heavy gold chain and studied the oval of jet. A carving of intertwined diamonds had been cut into the black stone. Softly glowing pearls outlined the jet motif.

'This pendant replaces your original one. How high you have risen, Marika. And how soon. Do you know why I chose you to become a member of the Discipline of Pearls?'

She shook her head.

'Because I saw myself in you. There is something cool, remote about you which is very appealing. But you have a deep sensuality coupled with the capacity to go after the things you want. You can be ruthless, at times – unpredictable. But you have proved that you'll accept any challenge. The society needs you, Marika. We need members who can be sent about society business. Members who will recruit those who are chosen by the elders.'

Marika slipped the pendant over her head. Perhaps she *was* like Stone in some ways. That would explain the strong physical attraction between them. Wasn't everyone looking for their twin self? And yes, she could be ruthless, even reckless, when necessary. It was a good thing that he knew that, because it might help him to understand what she was about to do. She felt calm and prepared.

Stone stood up and held out his hand. His little finger was held apart from the others, the pearl and jet ring presented for her kiss. She realised that she was expected to kneel and kiss his ring.

When she didn't move, his brows drew together. He watched her silently as she picked up her white kid handbag and put her hand inside. Finding what she was looking for, Marika picked up the black card and held it out to him.

Stone took it and stood looking down at the gold lettering.

'I won't kneel to you, Stone,' she said slowly and clearly. 'I submit to you on one count and one alone. My flesh is drawn to you, but my soul's my own. You won't ever own me, Stone. Next time we meet, you'll kneel to me.'

His dark eyes narrowed. For a moment she saw anger in their depths. Then they cleared and he smiled slowly. He nodded once, understanding perfectly. Glancing at the card once more, he slipped it into his jacket pocket.

'I accept the assignment,' he said coolly.

She'd known he would. The tension crackled between them.

'Unpredictable to the last. Touche, Marika. We'll meet again soon.' His voice held respect and did she detect the merest tremble of uncertainty?

That was a good enough beginning.

'The car's waiting outside,' she said evenly. 'I saw it from my room. Will you have my bags brought down?'

Marika turned and strode from the terrace. Pia would find the letter she had left, explaining everything. She would be in touch in due course. As she walked to the front door, the pendant swayed against her breasts.

Her hand came up to stroke the carving. A new phase of her life was about to begin. She had learned so much about herself. Part of that was down to Stone, but now *he* had some lessons to learn.

She was going to enjoy teaching him.

Lust Under Leo

Maria Lyonesse

'His rough tongue snaked around her nipple, showing no mercy. Where a moment ago he had been calculating, keeping her dangling on a line, now he was all joyful, animal lust.'

Jenna is enjoying her affair with her married boss Nick, until he throws a weekend-long thirtieth birthday party at a country hotel, and invites his wife Lisette, his sister Heather, and several important business colleagues. Lisette seems to share Nick's passion for Jenna, while innocent Heather is led astray by a handsome waiter with a penchant for motorbikes and leather. And overseeing the party, desiring, and desired by, all, is the enigmatic Robin.

Caught between business and pleasure, Jenna attempts to maintain a professional façade, while those around her toss theirs aside and give in to sensual indulgence. However, Nick's power is not as strong as he thinks and his past is about to make a takeover bid he hasn't bargained for . . .

Fanning the Fantasy

Zara Devereux

'Her pulse was thudding and she permitted her wandering hand to stroke his denim-clad thigh. Oh, she'd enjoy seducing this one, teaching him how to pleasure her and master the refined sensual delights she desired . . .'

Recently widowed Heather Logan is concerned about her sex life. It has always been unsatisfactory but now alone and inexperienced, Heather fears she will never find fulfilment.

Until a friend recommends Tostavyn Grange, a therapy centre for sexual inhibition. Their methods may be 'unconventional' but after some eye-opening preliminary sessions, Heather progresses in leaps and bounds and soon her deepest fantasies are coming true . . .